SECRET SUMMER

Stella Foster went to the village of Lange in Provence to carry out historical research for her thesis. When she met an attractive man who introduced himself as Professor Martin de Croix from the University of St Ayr, Stella thought there was something mysterious about him. She rang her friend, Sophie, at the University, who told her that no-one by the name of de Croix worked there. Who is this intriguing man, and just why is he in Lange?

HELEN McCABE

LP

SECRET SUMMER

Complete and Unabridged

LINFORD
Leicester

First published in Great Britain

First Linford Edition
published 1997

Copyright © 1992 by Helen McCabe
All rights reserved

British Library CIP Data

McCabe, Helen, *1942 –*
Secret summer.—Large print ed.—
Linford romance library
1. Love stories
2. Large type books
I. Title
823.9′14 [F]   23- 005339

ISBN 0–7089–5121–X

Published by
F. A. Thorpe (Publishing) Ltd.
Anstey, Leicestershire

Set by Words & Graphics Ltd.
Anstey, Leicestershire
Printed and bound in Great Britain by
T. J. International Ltd., Padstow, Cornwall

This book is printed on acid-free paper

1

STELLA took out her comb and tidied her unruly curls. She felt windblown and breathless after the exertion of cycling almost the whole way up the narrow street which led to the church. Then she turned to look at the view.

Below were red cliffs and wooded gorges, bright in the tawny evening sun. She could see the glint of the wide river as it meandered through the landscape. Above her, St Michel's spire could be seen for miles. It guarded the village of Lange, one of the prettiest in Provence.

Stella breathed deeply. The air was fresh, so different from the fumes of Parisian traffic; so peaceful after the pervasive noise in her small flat in St Germain's Latin Quarter.

"*Bonsoir, Mamselle!*" An old woman,

her head covered in a black scarf, greeted Stella as she pushed her bike through the iron gates of the church. The woman had evidently been visiting one of the graves in the lovingly-kept cemetery.

"*Bonsoir, Madame!*" Stella called back.

She was lucky, she mused, to be able to carry on with her historical research in Lange; lucky too, that her mother's friend, Catherine, had offered Stella a room for as long as she wanted in her house, standing right in the village square.

In fact, the summer had been more like a lovely dream than hard work. While Stella had wandered around the Roman arena and the magnificent baths at Nimes, she had almost forgotten that she was supposed to be finishing her thesis on the Roman occupation of Provence. All she seemed to have done was revel in the views, the scent of roses and geraniums and the beauty of hillsides covered with orange, lemon and olive groves.

Now, she had come to her senses. She had to, staying with the realistic Catherine, the epitome of French logic and sophistication. Her mother's friend seemed able to combine her love of painting with down-to-earth common sense and Stella could understand why the two women got on so well. She, herself, was liable to let her emotions get the better of her sometimes.

Her mother was much more level-headed. She and Catherine had been penfriends since childhood and had exchanged many holidays. When Catherine returned to the village where she had been born, to concentrate upon her painting, Stella's mother had been very eager for her daughter to visit Catherine before she left the Sorbonne.

Stella had agreed it was a marvellous idea until Provence, and Lange in particular, had lured her into spending carefree days without concentrating on her work.

That was why she had cycled up the hill on such a glorious summer evening. It had been almost a punishment for her laziness. It was to be part of her work also.

The church stood on the highest point and would give her a chance to look at the terrain. The hill itself had been an old Roman camp before Christianity and must have been rich with antiquities.

She had decided to visit the priest as well. He had been in the parish for many years and was said to be a scholar. Stella had found all this out in the small library and fixed it in her mind as she leaned her bike against the rough stone wall, trying to ignore the caress of the breeze which wafted in, touching her face with the lighest kiss.

She chained up her bike and made her way round the back of the church towards the presbytery and small hall. She glanced up to the roof, noting the leering eyes of several ugly gargoyles, deprived of rain by the wonderful summer weather.

Suddenly, another aroma made her head whirl, unmistakably French — wine and garlic were floating towards her from the hall. Stella smiled. It seemed the scholar priest was as fond of his wine as his books. She was looking forward to meeting him when she knocked on the heavy door, thinking that the priest would surely be able to tell her a lot about the history of the area.

"Yes?"

The door scraped open. Stella found herself staring through the gap into questioning brown eyes, framed by glasses. The priest and a blonde woman were seated at a polished table beyond, faces as blank as the man at the door.

"I beg your pardon," she began, "I didn't want to disturb you. I was looking for the parish priest . . . " She could see him rising from his chair.

"Really?" the man said, opening the door wider.

His eyes were piercing sharp behind the fashionable glasses. Suddenly, Stella realised she was noting how good-looking he was.

"Yes, but I'll go if I've disturbed something of importance."

She was embarrassed by such close scrutiny. The priest had risen from his seat, was standing, hands thrust down upon the table. With a shock, she realised his look was openly hostile. He was staring at her. She suddenly felt very uncomfortable and extremely unwelcome.

"I'd better go," she decided.

Suddenly, the woman was on her feet, too. She was slim and blonde, dressed casually in check shirt and jeans.

"Please, no, mademoiselle, come in," she urged. "You have disturbed nothing except a trivial meeting. We were looking at some ancient plans, that is all. We shall be finished soon!"

"Thank you," Stella replied.

"Père Cathé will be ready immediately.

Is it a pressing matter?"

"I was hoping to learn something of the church's history," Stella began as the woman led her across the room.

"Ah!" the man who had opened the door declared, walking in front of them. "Sit down!" He motioned to a vacant chair.

Stella sat uncomfortably, knowing from the atmosphere that, in spite of what they said, she had disturbed this strange little group for some reason. Now all she could do was lean back and listen to the discussion. The priest had not even acknowledged her presence. Stella was wondering whatever she would say to him when the discussion was over. He looked most unapproachable.

The younger man glanced at her.

"You're a stranger to Lange then? A tourist?"

"I'm staying in the village. Stella Foster."

"Martin de Croix." The words were low.

"Professor de Croix," the woman added swiftly. "From the University of St Ayr."

"Really?" It was Stella's turn to be surprised. St Ayr! The woman had been trying to impress her and she had managed it. What a coincidence! Stella's friend, Sophie, had been working there for four years. She would probably know him. "What subject, Professor?" Stella asked him in an interested voice.

"French History."

The reply was short. She could tell he didn't want to talk shop, so, while they continued to speak to one another, Stella was trying to remember hearing about Martin de Croix in that Department. Perhaps he was new. St Ayr had a reputation of attracting fine brains. The others proceeded with their conversation, but Stella could feel they were holding back. They had a map before them. Stella, reading it upside down, could see it was an ancient plan of the Château Lange.

8

As she was not brought into the conversation again, Stella began to observe her companions more closely. The woman had an air of fragility. She must have been beautiful once, but her looks were fading. Stella estimated she was in her late forties. She had seen trouble, because there was an air of sadness about her, Stella concluded. Yet when she was explaining some part of the plan's layout, the woman's excitement mounted. She reminded Stella of one of their Paris lecturers, who was always stirred when speaking of something which particularly interested him.

Martin de Croix did not have much to say. She wondered why not. The French found qualifications impressive and a small village like Lange would certainly have welcomed anyone like him. Why didn't his two companions give him the chance to air his views?

And what was he doing at a church meeting? What did the church have to do with the château? His face was a

9

little flushed. Stella knew academics very well and guessed that these two were on the brink of a find or had some other common interest.

Well, Professor de Croix, Stella thought, you're very attractive and young to be a Prof. He had a most aristocratic mouth and nose, a fine-boned face and his clothes were extraordinarily expensive even for Southern France.

She shut her eyes thinking of the name, de Croix. She had written a paper two years ago on French genealogy. She was trying to remember coming across the name — he had to be an aristocrat with that look.

She gave up after she had been through all the 'Cs' she could remember.

What about the priest? He had character written all over his old face. He looked like a scholar, with his shiny, bald head and gold-rimmed spectacles.

There was no warmth about him, however. He seemed as cool as the night breeze which was blowing about the hill top. His eyes were sunken; the skin stretched over his cheekbones so tightly it looked like it might tear. He reminded Stella of a mediaeval ascetic from her history books.

He glanced up suddenly and caught her staring. She lowered her eyes, listening carefully. It was all so mundane. She had been hoping to hear something more interesting than the details of the wine cellars of the Château Lange. She looked at the bottles on the table. So far no-one had offered her a drink even though they all had a glass before them. The priest saw her staring at the wine but ignored her.

So much for Provençal hospitality, she thought. I should have stayed with Catherine this evening!

The woman was leaning back. She picked up her glass, then she pushed a corner of the map towards Stella. At least it was some acknowledgement of her presence.

"This is quite an old parish," the

woman remarked. "Would you like to see?"

"Thank you," Stella replied. "I would be interested in looking at the map."

She bent over, feeling three pairs of eyes piercing her. When she lifted her head, they were all drinking their wine.

"Let's get on," de Croix urged. "Now, what about the other parts of the cellar?"

For some reason, the young professor was fascinated by the Château Lange's cellars. They started talking about measurements and area. What on earth were they looking for, Stella wondered. Treasure, perhaps? A more ill-assorted band of treasure hunters could scarcely be imagined. Again, Stella had the feeling they resented her being there. The woman was rattling off facts like a guide book. Suddenly, the professor poured out a glass of red wine and handed it over the table to her.

"Oh, thank you," she said.

"I hope you enjoy it, Miss Foster."

The woman was looking at her suspiciously as she spoke, so Stella leaned back and sipped the drink.

She began to plan what she would do tomorrow. She would cycle down to the little library and find out who built the château and who lived there now. As the woman took another sip of wine, Stella decided to give them something else to think about.

"I'm finding this really interesting, Professor," she remarked. "I'm researching in history myself. That's why I'm in Lange, so I'm not a tourist. By the way, I've a friend at St Ayr, Sophie Manche. You must know her!" Stella saw with surprise that beads of sweat were forming on his forehead.

"No, I don't think so." The dark eyes were expressionless as he took off his glasses and polished them. He looked much younger and more handsome without them.

"Surely you do? She's studying French History." To Stella's amazement he turned away towards the blonde, who was now standing.

"Mamselle Chard-Montaigne is about to leave!" The priest was directing his words to Stella. The woman inclined her head, turned away and went out of the door.

"We're finished now," Martin de Croix told Stella.

"I regret that I have no time to speak with you, mamselle," the priest said. "I have duties to perform." He was buttoning his soutane.

Stella was blazing angry. The last thing she'd expected from a priest was such rudeness. She picked up her bag, for she could see they were waiting for her to leave. She felt the hostile atmosphere again and could not understand.

"I beg your pardon, mamselle, but I must go," the priest told her. He turned swiftly, making for a back door which seemingly led into the church, for Stella caught the unmistakeable musty smell of age and incense. Not quite sure of what to do, she walked to the door. De Croix followed her.

"Au revoir, Miss Foster," he said. She was surprised he had even bothered to speak to her. Then he laid a hand on her arm. "I'm sorry Père Cathé is busy. Perhaps another time?"

"I don't think so," Stella replied. How could he be so rude one minute and polite the next? "I'm sorry I disturbed you."

"Did you drive here?"

"No, I have my bike!"

"What a pity. I could have given you a lift." When Stella didn't reply, he added, "I am sorry your journey was wasted."

"On the contrary, I found it most informative!" She saw a startled look cross his face for a moment and wondered why. Suddenly, the door to the sacristy opened. The old priest was standing there, watching them.

"Au revoir," she said lightly, but she could feel their eyes upon her. Then de Croix turned and walked over to the curé.

Below, the village lights were twinkling as she bent to unlock the chain, the shadowy branches of the trees waving in the dusk. Stella shivered. She mounted her cycle and wobbled through the gates into the street, making for the bright street lights at the bottom. Suddenly, she heard a car engine behind her. She flew down the hill, afraid to look back.

The noise grew louder. Stella had to brake and let the car go by. As the Citroën went past, she caught a glimpse of Mamselle Chard-Montaigne at the wheel, and Martin de Croix in the passenger seat.

★ ★ ★

"I've no idea who the man is," Catherine said, "but the woman's Céline Chard." She carried the dishes to the sink where Stella was washing up.

"Who is she?"

"The Countess's niece — from the

16

Château Lange!"

"Then that's why they were so respectful to her," Stella said.

"Old habits die hard in these villages," Catherine replied, smiling. "You wouldn't think there'd been a Revolution. The Chards all managed to escape Madame Guillotine — but not the Nazis!"

Stella put down the mop and stared at her hostess.

"What do you mean?"

"The poor girl's father and mother were shot by them."

"How horrible!"

"Yes, it was. The Chards were leading lights in the Resistance." Catherine had a faraway look in her eyes as she said it. Stella knew she was thinking about the war.

"You knew them?"

"Yes, they were good people. The Countess is nothing like her twin."

"How do you mean?"

"They were twins, the Countess and her brother. They say she was always

17

jealous of him — terrified he would inherit everything because he was male. When the Germans cracked down on the Resistance she didn't do anything to save him. She only cared about the Château.

"They promised not to set it on fire if she collaborated and gave away the names of the other members. None of them escaped — except her. She's had to live with knowing the whole village despises her, though. There was scarcely a family who didn't lose somebody." Bitterness had crept into Catherine's voice.

"Did you . . . ?" Stella didn't know how to finish the sentence.

"I lost my uncle. I was only seven but I'll never forget how we had to go to the town square and . . . "

"Don't!" Stella said. "I didn't mean to pry."

"Forty years is a long time for a village to ostracise anyone, but people round here still hate her. And that's why she hardly ever goes out alone;

no-one ever goes into the Château. As for Céline, no wonder she has never forgiven her."

"Then why does she live there?"

"She doesn't. She only visits. After all, when her aunt dies it will be hers."

"Quite a story," Stella said, seeing the blonde in a new light. "I suppose Céline's on holiday, but you know, Catherine, if I was her I wouldn't go and stay with any aunt who'd done that to my father."

"No doubt she has her reasons," Catherine said.

"And what about the professor? What's he doing in Lange?"

"Perhaps he's on holiday as well?"

"It must be a busman's holiday then, like mine!" Stella smiled, thinking about his serious face. "I wonder what the priest has to do with him? He looked really forbidding!" A smile came to Catherine's face then.

"Ah, Père Cathé has been here since the Thirties. He spent the whole war in this parish. He has seen enough to make a saint despair."

"No wonder he doesn't like strangers," Stella said thoughtfully.

"He hated the Germans. It was a wonder they didn't execute him. Fortunately the commandant was a good Catholic!"

Stella glanced at Catherine's grim face. "I'm sorry if I've hurt you by all these questions. You'll be wishing I hadn't come!"

"No, I won't. After all, if I can't make my dear old friend's daughter welcome in Provence, it'd be a pity." Stella was delighted to get off the subject of the war and talk about her mother.

They talked for a long time. When they had finished, Stella sat out in the garden and listened to the croaking bull frogs calling to her from the pond at the end of the walled garden. What Catherine had told her had been horrifying. It was hard to imagine that in such a quiet little village terrible things like that had happened.

"What are you thinking?" Catherine asked as she joined her in the garden.

"Just that what you told me was like a story, hardly believable on a night like this." The older woman looked up into the dark sky, letting the warm breeze ripple through her hair.

"Yes, I know, but it's all true. But it's history now."

"Everything's history, isn't it? Even what we said a moment ago. That's what I like about it; that's why I want to study it. Do you know what I'm going to do tomorrow?"

"What?"

"I'm going down to the library to find everything out I can about the Château Lange."

"Rather you than me! I'm going to get on with my painting."

"Thank you again for inviting me, Catherine."

"That's all right." The older woman laid a hand on her arm. "Whenever I've visited your mother in England,

I've had a wonderful time. I'm only repaying her, and I'm glad of the company."

"I'm glad you live in a lovely village like Lange and not in Lyons or Toulouse."

"Yes, Lange is truly beautiful." The golden moon was reflected in the pond, making the water a burnished gold on that summer night. At the water's edge, Catherine's white ducks were sleeping peacefully.

"The garden probably looked like this in the Middle Ages," Stella remarked.

"You're probably right. Especially the plumbing!" They laughed and walked back into the house.

As Stella closed the shutters in her room she looked across the square away from the church to where the dim shadow of the great house rose against the moon. The red rocks on which it stood were steep and covered with trees. It looked like a fortress and Stella closed her eyes, thinking of the horror it had seen. She imagined the old Countess lying awake, counting her sins. She shuddered a little, happy to climb into her bed where she could think about the three strange people she had met in the church hall.

★ ★ ★

Still mulling over Catherine's story, Stella wheeled her bicycle down the main street. Lange was awake and bustling with life. Stella loved the noise of the market that woke up the village at an unearthly hour. No wonder the inhabitants took a nap at noon.

The square was no longer empty. There were stalls everywhere. She had said last night that Lange was almost mediaeval, and it still had that timeless air. Awnings flapped in the breeze, hens squawked, dogs barked and French street cries echoed through the glittering air of early morning.

She was surprised to see Arabs with their wares spread out on the ground, bags and belts, pottery and necklaces.

One grinned as she passed, trying to catch hold of her handlebars, but she evaded him.

She wondered if anyone bought their goods as there were hardly any tourists this far off the usual routes.

The library was opening as she leaned her bike against its wall. Stella studied the plan. She would make for the local collection; request some documents about the Château. She got her student card ready and her university ticket. The woman at the desk looked, smiled and nodded her on her way.

She climbed up some twisting stairs towards the room where they kept the books about the village. Stella pushed open the swing doors, entering into a cool, cave-like room. She gasped. There, seated beneath the arched window, his head buried in a book, was Martin de Croix. He didn't even look up as she passed him on her way to the desk.

When she had looked in the catalogue

and found what she wanted, she filled in a sheaf of papers. Handing them to the librarian she was surprised to see him shake his head.

"I am sorry, mamselle, these are being looked at by the gentleman over there."

"What? All of them?"

"I'm afraid so. This is a small collection. We have no duplicates."

"Very well. I'll come back later," Stella said loudly. Martin de Croix looked up. For one moment she thought she saw sympathy in his eyes. Then he looked down again, ignoring her. She had been naive to hope he might allow her to read some of them, she thought, as she looked at the pile of books in front of him.

Twice now he had been insufferably rude. Just who does he think he is? she thought angrily as she walked back down the stairs and through the dark foyer into the noisy street.

In front of her the small café beckoned invitingly. She walked over, sat down under an umbrella and ordered lemonade. As she sucked on the straw her thoughts were full of Professor de Croix. Just why was he in Lange? What big attraction did the Château hold for him? What had he to do with the priest and Céline Chard? Still mulling this over, Stella finished her drink and went inside the café towards the pay phone. She had already made up her mind what to do.

She had to wait some time before she got through to Sophie.

"Stella! What a surprise! You're lucky you caught me. I was just going out!"

"Listen carefully, Sophie, this is important."

"What's the matter? You sound in a flap."

"No just a bit angry, that's all!"

"Oh?" Sophie sounded surprised.

"What do you know about Martin de Croix?"

"Who?"

"You must know him. Professor de Croix. French History at St Ayr — "

"I don't!"

"What do you mean?"

"I mean there's nobody in the French Faculty called that!"

"There must be!"

"No, I know them all. I would after four years, wouldn't I?"

"Is he new, do you think?"

"Well, whatever he is, he seems to have you guessing!" her friend said. "Look, I'll go and get the departmental brochure . . . " Stella hung on, counting her change. She heard Sophie run back. "Listen — Artur, Bering, Herene . . . " Sophie read them all out. "No de Croix, I told you. Anyway, I've never heard of him, have you?"

"No, I haven't!" It was dawning on Stella that the man seated over there in the library was an imposter. "Thanks, Sophie, I'm sorry to bother you. See you around."

"Sure. And I tell you, there's no de Croix. What does he look like? Anyway, Stella, why are you so interested? Is he — " Stella was suddenly glad she had no more change because Sophie was so intent on knowing every last little detail.

"Thanks! Bye!" she said. There was silence. She picked up her bag, walked from the booth, deep in thought. Questions flooded her brain. What was going on in Lange? Who was this man masquerading as a professor? What had he to do with the mysterious and tragic Céline Chard? And the priest?

She was going to be around Lange for quite a time. She would go back to the church on the hill, even up to the Château Lange if she had to, because whatever happened she was going to get to the bottom of this mystery . . .

2

THE Château Lange certainly has a gruesome history! Stella thought as she turned over the pages of the books which had been returned to the desk in the small library.

She had seen the mysterious 'Martin de Croix' leave in a smart convertible and would have loved to follow him. No chance, she'd thought, looking at her old bike regretfully. So she had taken his place in the dim library and begun to read.

It was a bloodthirsty tale. The Chards had been Lords of the Manor since mediaeval times and had left their mark. There were accounts of floggings; even a report of the public execution of some poor serf who had failed to please his cruel master; tables of repression, which could not even be equalled by the bloody Revolution that was to come in the eighteenth century.

However, when she reached the records of the Second World War, she found there was a kinder Chard in power. She swallowed when she read about the Nazi Occupation and the horrific incident which Catherine had recounted the night before. History had certainly been cruel to the people of Lange. She was glad she could look out on a calm, sunlit village square instead of red flags fluttering, emblazoned with ugly swastikas.

Finally, she pored over the Château's layout, the ornamental gardens and lake, the bird sanctuary — and held her breath when she learned of the legend that existed about an ancient secret passageway through which the Chards had escaped from the Revolution. It was reputed to begin in the wine cellars — and that was the area in which the strange trio in the Church Hall were particularly interested.

She wondered if that was what they had been discussing so eagerly when her appearance on the scene had caused them to clam up. After a long, stuffy afternoon inside, Stella closed the books, went downstairs, unchained her bike and returned to Catherine's house.

"Catherine?" Stella was lingering over a fine pork cutlet, laced with piquant garlic. "Do you think there's any chance that I could look around the Château Lange?"

"It might be difficult," her friend replied. "The Countess doesn't like visitors."

"Do you know her personally?"

"A little, but I don't like her."

"So you said."

"But I know her secretary very well!" Catherine laughed.

"Really?" Stella hoped that the eagerness would not show too much in her voice.

"Yes, Johann is a good friend of mine."

"Johann?"

"Oui, don't be surprised that the Countess' secretary is a man. She doesn't get on with women. He's a local. He suits her — he is erudite and businesslike. He is also half-German. He has no time for the past, as he calls it, and the Countess pays very well!" Catherine shrugged her shoulders in an extravagant French gesture which meant everything. "The Germans did leave some good things behind them."

Stella would have loved to know what kind of relationship existed between Catherine and Johann, but she resisted the impulse to ask her anything else about him. It seemed that this showed in her face, because in the next breath Catherine added:

"We have an understanding, that's all. I'll do what I can. I'll tell Johann you have an historical interest in the place and leave it to him — "

* * *

32

Several days later, the invitation came, brought by Johann himself. Catherine's friend was thick-set and blond, but had a merry, intelligent look with the well-cut clothes and sophisticated aura of a born Frenchman.

"There you are, Kate, your friend is in luck. Mme la Comtesse is amenable — she'll let Stella go round. She's entertaining already — Mamselle Céline — and they don't get on. Therefore, she needs some entertainment." He smiled disarmingly at Stella, who thought again just how charming some Frenchmen were.

"Thank you, Jo!" Catherine said — and kissed him.

"Thank you, Johann," Stella added, "but when?" She could hardly wait.

"Monday." He offered her the note. "But remember not to be late. She hates unpunctual people. And you are invited for coffee!" He winked, turning to Catherine. "The old girl's really lonely. Now, don't say she deserves it! She knows what the locals think

33

of her — so she makes her friends elsewhere. She's quite an intellectual, Stella, so be ready for some piercing questions!"

"I will," Stella answered, delighted.

In the next few days, she wandered about the village, reading — and hoping that she might see one of the trio who had started off her interest in the Château Lange. But Stella was disappointed. 'Martin de Croix' had simply vanished. Where was he staying? Perhaps he was Père Cathé's guest? Could he be staying at the Château? After all, he had left with Céline Chard!

Monday dawned warmer than ever. The sun, which was already scorching the bare bodies of his worshippers on the Mediterranean coast, flooded the village of Lange, waking it with brilliant light, making the Château above look even more unapproachable. Catherine had offered to take her up in the car, but Stella wanted to arrive alone.

"I'll walk the rest of the way,

Catherine," Stella said glancing up, "unless, of course, you want to see Johann."

"No, we had plenty to say to each other last night," her friend replied. Stella wasn't sure if the older woman's friendship with Johann was becoming a little strained because of her presence. The two of them had entertained him to dinner the night before and Stella had felt uncomfortable. It didn't seem right playing gooseberry on that warm Provençal night, when glittering fireflies danced and the bullfrogs croaked across from the village pond. Besides Stella had been thinking about 'Martin de Croix' again and why he had wanted to deceive people.

"You're sure you don't want to see Johann?"

"Quite!"

"Then I'll get out. It isn't that hot and it'll save the Renault negotiating those hairpin bends." In fact, Stella was a little nervous about the way Catherine always seemed so near the edge of the mountain roads.

"All right. It will save me turning at the top. Just ring the bell of the gatehouse."

★ ★ ★

The whole Château appeared to spread across the flat top of the red cliff, the twin to the one on which Père Cathé's church stood — in fact, the 'Twins of Lange' were what the locals called the two mountains. The back of the Château's hill undulated towards the lake and those gardens housed small and precise waterfalls which fed the fountain.

It, in turn, spewed the tame torrents into the man-made lake. The Château's grounds were surrounded by a wall, which stretched east and south. In fact, the whole domain seemed closeted from the outside world, ruled over by a mistress who hid herself away from local life.

Stella's hand trembled a little as she

pulled the iron bell rod. She held the letter of invitation in her other hand. She was nervous about meeting the Countess, but, beneath, her excitement was increasing.

There was no answer to her ring, so she stood back, surveying the stone work and the leaded windows of the lodge.

She was about to ring again when a voice said:

"Mamselle!" The tone was cold and precise. Stella turned and her eyes met the sunken ones of the old parish priest. He wasn't wearing his soutane, just a black suit and an open-necked black shirt, which revealed a thin white chest.

"Père Cathé," she greeted him carefully.

"There's no-one to answer you, Mamselle Foster." She knew he was telling her not to bother.

"They will, mon Père. I've been invited." He inclined his head stiffly, but the look in his eyes was hot and piercing.

"How interesting for you." Now the tone was scornful.

"Yes, I think it will be," Stella countered, moving towards the door. Suddenly, he stepped forward and rested his hand on her arm.

"Be careful, mamselle, the Countess does not welcome inquisitive visitors."

"I beg your pardon?" Stella said, wondering if she had misheard. Why was he so insulting?

"Oui, mamselle, the Countess has never made guests welcome." Stella shivered. Why didn't he go back to his church, which was as cold as he was?

"I'll remember that, Père Cathé," she replied, feigning carelessness. She turned towards the bell. He was already striding off. After, he paused at a small arched gate set into the Château wall. She watched him try it, then hurry off down towards the village.

Feeling most uncomfortable, she rang again. Perhaps no-one would answer. Had Johann made a mistake? Why didn't Père Cathé want her visiting the Château? What was he doing there anyway and why had he tried the gate in the wall? Just then she heard a key in the lock and bolts being withdrawn. The noise was followed by a woman's voice:

"I am sorry, mamselle, that I didn't come sooner, but I was up at the house when I heard the bell." With relief, Stella saw the speaker was a smartly dressed woman. She'd half-expected to see some old retainer out of a horror movie.

Then the gates of the Château Lange closed behind her and she was ushered through the dark archway of the gatehouse into the brilliant sunlit courtyard beyond . . .

The Countess didn't seem sinister in the least. She wore shantung and pearls which complemented an elegant grey hairstyle, formed into a neat French pleat. She appeared very pleased to entertain Stella and enthused about the Château's treasures, insisting on showing her all the priceless porcelain and the Louis Quatorze dinner service.

Of Céline, there was no sign — until coffee. Stella was seated, balancing an exquisite cup of white wafer-thin china and attempting to answer some questions about Roman civilization, when the door opened to reveal the Countess' niece.

"Entrez, Céline." It was the Countess' use of the verb that startled Stella. She did not use the familiar 'tu' for her niece. Then Stella noticed the old lady's expression. She had begun to believe that the Countess might have been much maligned.

She seemed so civilised and pleasant, Stella had wanted to forget about the terrible betrayal during the Nazi Occupation; but, on Céline's entrance, she seemed to catch a glimpse of the Countess' other self. There was open unpleasantness on her patrician face — terrible dislike — even hatred?

"This is Mamselle Foster, my guest for the morning. She is an historical researcher. Her afternoon is up to you.

Make of it what you will!"

Stella thought that Céline would acknowledge her and refer to their earlier meeting in the church hall, but she did not. She only extended her hand in a haughty manner and uttered the usual politenesses. Suddenly, Stella sensed she shouldn't mention their meeting. She knew that Céline was warning her against it.

Yet there was so much coldness on the Frenchwoman's part; Stella felt she resented her being at the Château as much as at the church. It was the most uncomfortable coffee break that Stella could ever remember. The two women continued being openly sarcastic to each other. She just had to put an end to it. She finished her coffee.

"That was lovely. Thank you. Will it be possible for me to see the lower floors and the gardens?"

"Céline is free to show you," the Countess replied with a note of dismissal. "It was enchanting to meet you!" However polite the words,

Stella recognised the hollowness in the tone.

* * *

Céline spoke very little as she led Stella from room to room. She, too, appeared to have her mind on something more important. Added to this, she continually glanced at her watch, but Stella hung on stubbornly. Should she mention the church meeting? Ask about the legend of the passage? She decided.

"It's been a wonderful morning, Mamselle Chard-Montaigne, but I'm awfully interested in something I read about in the town library. I didn't hear you mention it that night in the church hall. About a secret passage leading from the cellars? Does it really exist?" She hadn't counted on the effect this would have on Céline. The woman stopped in her tracks and stared. A dull redness was coming to her cheeks.

"I have no idea, Miss Foster."

"But you seem to know so much about the Château. Surely Professor de Croix — " Céline glanced at her watch again.

"I'm sorry, but I have to go. Feel free to wander about the gardens. Don't forget to look at the bird sanctuary. My aunt keeps some exotic species in the aviaries — and, when you've finished, just call on Madame Blois and she will see you out. Once again, my apologies. Good-afternoon!" She walked away, leaving Stella to feel embarrassed and angry.

She told herself off for being so unsubtle, but it was quite clear that whatever was going on the strange trio were keeping it to themselves. What else did she expect? She was an outsider with no business being there.

She wasn't usually so persistent or inquisitive. It was just the way they had treated her. It made her see red — and added to that, why was someone masquerading as a university professor?

There was no doubt about it. Something very strange was going on. Céline Chard knew about the legend — but she wasn't prepared to talk about it. Why did everyone try to fob Stella off with weak excuses? And just where did 'de Croix' fit into it all?

Racking her brains, Stella sauntered by the side of the lake, watching the pretty ducks diving into the water, listening to the sound of the doves in the gardens, letting the hot sun bore into her shoulders. She pushed back some escaping curls under her broad headband and sat down to think, hidden in the shadow of a sweet scented profusion of bougainvilleas.

Then she heard voices. They were coming from the direction of a small summerhouse. Stella sat up. She didn't care to eavesdrop, but she wanted to see who could be visiting the Château unannounced.

She approached, keeping in the shadows. The man's voice was raised;

44

it was deep and gruff with a guttural Southern accent.

"You fool! She must be looking, too!"

"How could she be? Anyway, I told her nothing!"

The woman's voice was instantly recognisable. It belonged to Céline Chard. Stella's face blazed. They must be speaking of her!

"She has something to do with him. I know it! If anything happens now — " he growled.

"Please, Henri, don't shout! I'm doing my best. I really am! I couldn't stop her coming here today. It wasn't my fault. It was arranged by the secretary!"

"Blast the Kraut!" He spat out the words — and Stella still couldn't see their faces.

"I tell you, it wasn't my fault!" Stella knew Céline was afraid of the man's anger. Could it be 'de Croix' — but he didn't speak with that accent.

"Well, make sure she's safely off the

place before this evening. I'm warning you. If anything goes wrong, I'll — "

"All right! I understand." Céline was pleading now. Stella was dying to know what was going to happen later! She had to find out!

The voices ceased. Stella stepped sideways quickly so she wouldn't be discovered. Then she tripped over something — and someone who was directly behind her. She fell backwards with a gasp and to her horror felt a hand clamp over her mouth and stifle the scream that was forming in her throat.

Then his strong arms were pulling her back into the undergrowth.

She realised he wished to be discovered even less than she did. She struggled helplessly, looking backwards into the handsome face of 'Martin de Croix'. On the other side, footsteps were passing close by — and disappearing. He lifted his hand from her mouth, leaving her trembling and angrily rubbing her bruised arms. She stared at him from terrified eyes.

"Don't touch me again — or I'll scream!"

"Please don't," he said softly. "I didn't mean to hurt you — but I couldn't let them see us!" Stella was backing away.

He took off his glasses and wiped his forehead. He looked ashamed of his action, but Stella couldn't trust him.

"I'm going up to the house — " she began, although all she really wanted from him was some explanation of his monstrous behaviour. She knew she should shout for help and run, but she was stiff with shock.

"No, please," he begged, "don't do that. I can explain."

"You'll have to," Stella said. Her voice sounded as if it was coming from far away. It was high and unnatural with shock.

"Will you listen?"

"I'm listening." Stella tried to keep the fear out of her voice.

"If they'd found us — " he broke off. Stella knew he was looking for the right words. If she could just control herself a little longer, she would find out about the whole mysterious business.

"Who are 'they'? I thought one was Céline Chard — that you were friends with her, Professor." She had to call him that, so afterwards she could accuse him of lying.

He looked round.

"I can tell you nothing here. It isn't safe." She almost laughed. Who was he to be talking about safety? He had behaved like a madman. "Will you come to the summerhouse?"

"No, I won't," she shivered. She should stop talking and run — but she wanted to know so much!

"I promise I won't hurt you." He looked like an ordinary chap now, asking her to go for a walk.

"I can't believe you," she said.

"I know. I don't blame you after what I did, but there was a reason — a good one. It was a question of my future. I'm not what you think."

She looked at him steadily as he

48

waited for her reply.

"Who are you?" Stella asked simply. If he came clean, didn't lie this time, she might go with him and hear the rest.

"Why do you ask that? You know, don't you?"

"Goodbye, *Professor*!" She turned and walked away. She could hear him behind her.

"All right, I guess you know more than I think. I'll explain anything — but don't go up to the house and say you've seen me." Stella had the upper hand and she knew it. When she stopped, turned and looked into his eyes, she felt guilty that she'd made the man plead. All the arrogance he'd displayed in the church hall was past — whatever he was, or had done, he would do anything now for her co-operation.

"I'll come with you," she said, "but if you dare lay a finger on me, I'll scream until I bring everyone running."

"Thank you, Miss Foster," he said,

"you won't have to. I promise."

As they walked towards the little summerhouse, they didn't speak, but kept close under the shadow of the bushes.

Several times he looked over his shoulder and involuntarily quickened his pace, until they were close inside the white-painted structure with its glass windows overlooking the lake. Stella sat down on an ornamented cast-iron chair. She was trembling.

Part of her was saying she was a fool to take him at his word, but the intuitive part was telling her she had done right to trust him. Besides, she thought, looking at his face which was pale in spite of the tan, I'm attracted to you, 'Martin de Croix'. I know you're not a real villain. You look too honest for it now.

He swallowed:

"They won't come back. OK. I promised — " He breathed in. "I'm not sure where to start. I've never told this to anyone, let alone a stranger, but you just happened to come along at the wrong time — "

"The church hall?"

"Yes!" He flushed.

"Well," she said, finding her self-possession, "I suggest you tell me who you really are and why you've been masquerading as a professor from St Ayr."

To her surprise, he approached her, and put his hand on the arched back of the chair.

"That's just it, Miss Foster," he said. "I'm not masquerading as a Professor. I am one — from that very University!"

Stella swallowed, and looked round for some means of escape. He wasn't going to tell her the truth after all. Why had she been so foolish? She tried to stand up, but her legs were weak. He put out his hand and firmly pushed her back into the chair . . .

3

STELLA had never thought she would be in such a position. She had sometimes wondered what she would do if she had ever been threatened by a man, but she had never been able to make up her mind. At that moment she wished she had taken the lessons in self defence that she had been offered at University. There was nothing she could do now except scream. She opened her mouth.

"I wouldn't scream if I were you," he said quietly. He didn't look at all threatening and the push back into the chair hadn't been particularly violent, only firm.

"I won't, then, but you'd better tell me the whole story."

"All of it?" he replied and she was angry again because she was sure he was making fun of her. She liked the quizzical curl of the lip and the half-smile, but she was aggrieved.

"I don't think it's funny!" she retorted, looking down at her spoiled summer skirt. Then suddenly and for no reason, she wanted to smile too, but she decided against it. However, now she didn't feel frightened at all, only hot and somewhat bothered.

"You look fine," he said, his eyes following her glance at the skirt.

"No thanks to you then! Do you always treat women like that?"

"Never," he replied and she was sure it was the truth. "I do apologise, Miss Foster." He walked away from her chair and sat down himself in the corner of the summer-house. She remained uneasily on the chair, her hands smoothing down her skirt and picking off traces of grass. "That is true," he added. "And I am a professor. That's true as well."

"At St Ayr?" she accused. "You couldn't be. My friend, Sophie knows everyone and she's never heard of

Martin de Croix."

"All right," he replied, watching what she was doing. "I suppose I have to come clean, which is more than that skirt will do if you keep messing with it like that!"

She blushed.

"Go on. Amaze me with the truth!"

"Indeed I might just do that," he said, looking her directly in the eyes. She could see he wasn't joking.

"Carry on then. What is all this cloak and dagger stuff?" Stella realised just how sarcastic she sounded, but she couldn't help it because she had been so frightened initially and she didn't enjoy the feeling one little bit.

"I am not Martin de Croix," he said suddenly. Stella didn't like the confession at all. There was something sinister about masquerading as someone else.

"Does he even exist?" she asked, just to find something to say in answer to such bluntness.

"No, I chose de Croix because it

sounded good. Marcel is my real name."

"Well, how do you do?" Stella said. But she hadn't counted on his reaction. He jumped up, came over and kissed her hand. Her joke had quite backfired but the touch of his kiss was gentle and made her heart jump.

Whatever was she doing letting this man kiss her? She withdrew her hand smartly.

Marcel was looking, noticing how jumpy she was. Then she felt embarrassed.

"Go on," she urged.

"Marcel de Parais."

"That's an interesting name," she replied. He must have missed the disbelief in her voice because he was smiling.

"It's an old name, a very old name."

"Almost aristocratic?" She was really going a bit too far but he didn't seem to notice her banter at all. Could he really be Marcel de Parais? More likely it was another name he had invented.

"I'm afraid so. My grandfather was

the Comte de Parais." It sounded good, even if the Paris telephone directories were full of titles like that.

"And I suppose you're being pursued for a romantic reason?"

"Mamselle?" he looked uncomfortable and puzzled.

"I'm sorry," Stella said, "please carry on now you've started." But, suddenly he wasn't smiling.

"This is no joke, Miss Foster," he said, "even though the English make sport of most things. This is very serious." Stella was remembering the urgent voices of Céline Chard and her mysterious companion. Yes, that had been serious and she suddenly realised she was behaving too flippantly.

She knew nothing about what was going on and she was intrigued. She had to find out and, if being civil to Marcel de Parais was the price she had to pay, so be it.

Suddenly, Stella knew the young man was serious. She recognised that from the look he gave her. It was a

56

glance that seemed to say, "But can I trust you with what I'm going to tell you?" She knew that she wanted him to tell her what he was doing, what he meant to gain from posing as someone else?

It wasn't normal behaviour, but what was normal anyway? Stella herself wasn't behaving normally.

Marcel took off his glasses and passed a hand over his eyes as if he was tired. Stella waited, watching his nervous actions. You didn't have to be a psychology student to see that Marcel was hesitant in telling her the 'truth'. He replaced the spectacles and came over towards her chair. He pointed to another garden chair that was folded up and standing in the corner of the summer-house.

"One moment, Miss Foster. I'll just bring this over." She knew he was prevaricating. Still, she supposed he couldn't tell her everything seated on the floor! He drew the white-painted chair near to hers and settled himself.

"I hope no-one will find us here together," she said. "I'm supposed to be looking at the aviaries — and then going back to the village."

"Well, that's something," he replied. "At least you aren't afraid of me any more." The light remark showed he was feeling less tense.

"I really will have to go soon," she told him, "and you do owe me this explanation after grabbing me like that." Suddenly he began to laugh and, in spite of herself, she broke into laughter too.

"I assure you, Miss Foster, I am not in the habit of pouncing on young ladies." Stella felt her cheeks go quite hot.

"Please call me Stella," she said firmly. He gave a quick nod of acquiescence:

"And, please, I am Marcel?"

"I hope so." She smiled again. Marcel leaned back in the light chair and looked across the summer-house. His voice was quite soft at first and

Stella had to strain her ears to catch the first words of the story . . .

"What is left of the Château d'Artaigne is to the north-east of Lange village. It was the apex of a triangle, one point of which was the Château Lange, one that of Saint Michel . . . " He shook his head. "No, that's not right. I'll start again. There's so much to tell you and I'm not sure where I should begin . . . !"

"At the beginning?" Stella suggested gently.

"Go on, Marcel. The Château d'Artaigne? Tell me about it. I've never heard of it." He looked at her and she could see that his eyes were moist.

"*Non*, I am sure that you have never heard of it, Stella. There is nothing left of my home any more."

"Your home?" She didn't know what to expect.

"Yes but I have never lived there." She recognised the bitterness in his voice. "I wish I had. It was a lovely place. My father — " Marcel was

59

getting up from the chair and walking about the summerhouse. He turned to Stella, opening his hands in a gesture that showed his difficulty with words. Then he thrust his tanned hands into his pockets. "No, I'm not making much sense, am I? Here I am, a professor of history and I can't say a word."

"If it's too painful, I don't mind," Stella replied, wishing now she had never tried to find out the secret behind all this. She knew there must be something terrible on the Frenchman's mind and she sensed it was going to tie in with the macabre history of this pretty Provençal village. She waited while he controlled his emotions.

"The beginning, you said. All right, I'll try. One has to go very far back, Stella. You know that there was a Roman camp round here?"

"Yes," Stella replied eagerly, "that was how it all started. I'd come to ask Père Cathé if he knew much about the settlement."

"Père Cathé knows a lot about everything and not only the Romans. This region has had too many invaders." The words were brusque.

"You mean the war?"

"Just so."

"Catherine — where I'm staying — told me something about it."

"I see — then that may make things a little easier for you to understand." She thought he was being a trifle sarcastic, but he appeared entirely innocent of the charge as he continued, "We should go further back than the Thirties to understand about the Château d'Artaigne. Back to seventeen eighty-nine, in fact."

"The French Revolution?"

"Oui, Stella, a date everyone is able to remember. Of course, the Château d'Artaigne, like the Château Lange, had been standing a good four hundred years before then."

"Yes, I read about the history of Lange — when I got hold of the books." Stella just couldn't help being

61

a little sarcastic either.

"But there was nothing of Artaigne? Our Nazi friends saw to that. They intended to eradicate it from memory."

"Oh," Stella said, afraid of what was to come . . .

"Artaigne was an exceptionally pretty chàteau," he began. "It was built first in the old military style. Of course, the mediaeval walls had disappeared by then, because in the sixteenth Century, the lord of Artaigne decided to build on some turrets and spires.

"So Artaigne ended up a bit like a fairytale, with an ornamental lake in front and lovely meadows and woods behind.

"A small village grew about its walls but there was no church there for the villagers to go to. The lord had his own chapel in the Chàteau and, being a true aristocrat, kept it for himself and the family; therefore, the peasants had to walk the five miles to Lange and hear Mass at St Michel. The priest at Lange was the pastor of Artaigne.

"Lange and Artaigne always shared the priest and thus became very good friends. The two families were always close, and stayed close."

Marcel sat down again, calmer now he'd managed to get started.

"Think about that time, Stella. Not all peasants were against their masters and that was true in Artaigne at least. Both families could see the Revolution was coming, so Roger Parais, my ancestor, known as Roger d'Artaigne, had a very bright idea. He decided to build a passage — "

"A secret passage?"

"The very same," Marcel replied. "A passage which connected the two great houses. A wonderful passage, constructed by the peasantry and emerging in the thicket of the forest, as it was then — I'm afraid the forest has disappeared now.

"I feel that I can trust you, Stella, I must, or I wouldn't be telling you this."

She nodded. "You can trust me."

"Right. Back to Roger. He was a man of enormous ingenuity, but fairly vain and, I believe, given to sarcasm.

"He had a portrait painted of himself in mediaeval armour. They say its most striking feature was the eyes — very dark and brilliant. My father told me that they seemed to burn right through the portrait.

"Yes, Stella, all the lords of Artaigne have such eyes. But, anyway," he sighed, "I'm not making a great deal of headway and — it strikes me — I myself may be in a little danger sitting here in the summer-house telling you this story."

"Please don't stop now, Marcel," she cried, "we can keep a look out. I can see the path really well from here." Stella was walking across looking out through the glass. Marcel came and stood beside her.

"No, I won't stop, because I need your help, Stella." He put a hand on her arm and she was conscious of a tiny thrill. "You will help, I can sense it."

"Carry on, Marcel," she said, trying to make her voice quite normal, although all she could feel through her body was his touch.

"Anyway, in seventeen eight-nine, the aristoratic Roger and his friend, Montaigne, were ready. Their own villagers alerted them that the revolutionaries were on their way.

"Roger had all the valuables transferred to the passage, all the priceless things he wanted to leave and, of course, all the belongings and money he would need for his flight to England.

"Now, let's come back to the present. I have told you that my father was the Comte de Parais, I am Marcel de Parais, and that I lecture at St Ayr — your friend, Sophie, will confirm it. I am in this village under an assumed name because of what I have just told you. A few old people in Lange will still remember the Parais family and the history of the Artaigne Château, and I don't want that. Even your friend, Catherine, might remember.

I don't want my identity public as yet. I am actually staying with Père Cathé."

"With the priest?"

"Yes, he has been a very good friend to my family. He has also been a good friend to Lange."

"I know now why he's popular. Catherine says the villagers like him a lot and I couldn't understand it."

"I haven't told you yet."

"No, I suppose you haven't," Stella agreed. "But what about Cèline Chard? Where does she fit in?" Stella wanted to know.

"Has Catherine told you anything about the Countess?"

"I'm afraid so."

"Ah, then it'll be easier for me. So you will know why Céline was with Père Cathé and me that evening."

"Not really."

"You do know though that Céline doesn't get on with the Countess, her aunt?"

"How could she after what happened

66

during the war?" Marcel looked as if he agreed.

"Yes," he replied, "and, naturally, Céline was the only one who could get hold of the maps we needed. She had to do it on the quiet. Now I'll tell you what all this is about.

"I swear every word I'm going to tell you is the truth. It's not a very nice story and it's painful.

"I want you to try and imagine it's nineteen forty-three and there are Nazis crawling all over the place. The square at Lange is full of swastikas. The people want to pull them off the walls but they daren't. Five miles away is a very lovely chateau, standing here minding its own business just as it's done since the Middle Ages.

"There are lots of ducks swimming on the lake. They know nothing about Hitler. They're swimming and diving and the little boy watching doesn't know anything about what's going on in Lange. He's just watching the ducks." Marcel paused. "That boy was my father, Stella. He had the misfortune to be born into one of the bloodiest times the Château d'Artaigne had ever seen, in spite of all the wars it had weathered."

Stella nodded, remembering Catherine's story and how glad she'd been that now Lange, France and the Western World were at peace.

"I'll tell you all this just as my father told me. It'll be easier and you said you wanted to know."

"I do."

4

THE boy looked up and pulled a face. He was hoping they wouldn't come and fetch him because he was having a good time. Watching the ducks gave him a chance to get away from the house, where everyone seemed to be miserable. He wasn't used to that, because he'd been happy before. There was only one thing that Phillipe de Parais remembered being as bad as this — the day Maman had died. It had been awful but he could hardly remember it that much. He had been very small and his father had been in a terrible state, but he'd taken Phillipe away with him to the coast and they'd spent quite a long time walking on the beach and riding in the hills. He'd missed Maman a lot but he got over it.

This was different. He might be nine but he knew about the war. The Nazis were very bad people, but no-one would let him say so. If he said anything, someone would tell him to be quiet. The cook was always staring out of the window as if she was afraid. In fact, everyone seemed afraid — except Papa, of course. Papa wasn't frightened of anything.

He was the Comte de Parais and could do anything he wanted. The villagers really liked him and Phillipe was proud to be the heir. At first he hadn't understood that. Now he realised that all this, the Château, the lake, the ducks, absolutely everything would be his — after Papa was dead. But he didn't want to think about that.

"Phillipe, where are you?" It was his father's voice. Phillipe picked up a stone and flung it into the lake. Luckily, it missed a duck. Marcel wouldn't have wanted to hurt even one of them.

"I'm here, by the lake!"

"Phillipe!" His father's voice had an urgent sound about it. Phillipe sensed something was wrong, so he began to run. Why did his father want him? Why hadn't he sent the cook or the maid?

Then he saw them. Strangely, that moment stayed with him for years. There were three people coming to meet him. One was Papa; he was walking in the middle. The other two men were each side of him. They had steel grey uniforms and peaked caps.

Behind them the familiar turrets and spires of the chateau were like a picture beckoning him, but it felt like a dream. They were still walking towards him.

"Phillipe, come here. Don't be afraid." He was angry then not only because of what his father said, but because he must have been showing his fear. Phillipe stood quite still, feeling his heart beating fast, thumping madly under his jersey.

"Don't be afraid," his father repeated. Then Phillipe looked up at him and, with a sudden shock, saw that Papa was afraid as well! It was then that Phillipe felt his hands begin to shake a bit so he thrust them into his pockets.

"My son," the Count said, putting his arm about the boy's shoulders. Both soldiers gave a correct little nod of acknowledgement.

"Good!" the taller of the two said. "What a delightful son you have." The German was staring directly at Phillipe, who breathed in deeply and made a movement to get nearer his father. Papa returned the movement with the slightest pressure about his neck. Phillipe was conscious that the touch was telling him to be civil and careful to these men. He stood passively under the officer's gaze.

"Come," the man said and the four of them turned away from the glassy lake and the ducks . . .

There were more soldiers inside the Château. Two trucks were outside on the drive, one was filled with men wearing ugly grey helmets. They sat stiffly as the four walked slowly up the steps. Phillipe was hanging back, but the officer, who had spoken earlier, took his arm and guided him through the arched doorway under the shield that bore the arms of Artaigne. Phillipe looked to his father for comfort but the other soldier was walking with him across the hall in front of them.

What was to come was more unnerving. Inside the spacious drawing room the German soldiers had arranged for the servants to be present. Cook was there and the maids, even the gamekeeper from the estate — all standing, silent and afraid. There was a tense atmosphere and Phillipe could feel his own fear sliding out and merging with the others. It was a terrible afternoon.

"I am warning you, Count, you have four days in which to make up your mind. You will be well watched in the meantime. There will be guards in your grounds, who will take care to see that nothing is taken from the Château."

Phillipe swallowed the lump which had risen in his throat. The swallowing brought a gurgling noise and everyone stared at him. He would not cry! He blinked instead.

The officer came over and put a hand on his shoulder.

"The boy understands even if you do not, Count. He wants his heritage preserved. The Reich will be its protector. He also knows the penalty for not complying with the order."

There was nothing anyone could do. The soldiers had the upper hand. So this is what war meant. Phillipe was realising that, after all, his father was not the most powerful man in the whole world. The power lay with these sinister and cruel men in their black and grey uniforms.

When the officers had disappeared and the two trucks had roared away down the long drive, the Comte de Parais took his son's hand and drew him to his side. The servants stood waiting for orders.

"Well," he said, "you have all heard the ultimatum. Now I want you to start packing up," he told his staff.

"Where are we going to go, sir?" the cook cried, her face white and tears coming down her cheeks.

"You, my dear, will go back to Lange and stay with your sister."

"But what about you, sir? Who will cook for you and Master Phillipe?"

"We shall be all right. We are making plans already."

"What about us?" the gamekeeper asked, and the other servants nodded.

"I wouldn't have you hurt for the world and you will be if you remain loyal to me. You must save yourselves. I can assure you that, when the Nazis have taken what they want from my treasures, they will not be satisfied. You must find somewhere to go."

The Count released his hold on Phillipe's hand and went over to his desk. He took out his keys and opened a drawer. From it he took a wad of franc notes. He looked at the staff.

"I want you to take the money I give you. It is the best I can do for you all in the circumstances." Several of the maids were crying. Phillipe watched everything very carefully so that he would never forget it.

He was proud of his father, who was so calm. The Count handed out notes to each of his employees. When he reached the gamekeeper, Henri, Phillipe heard his father say something in a low voice and the man nodded in return. Then, like the other servants, he left the large room without looking behind him. Phillipe almost cried himself when Cook went. He had always liked the woman. She stopped on the way to give him a kiss.

"God bless you, Master Phillipe," she said and hurried out.

★ ★ ★

Later that evening the Count let Phillipe sit on his knee in front of the fire. Phillipe hadn't done that for a long time, but that night he wanted to be close to Papa.

"You understand what the Nazis want, don't you, Phillipe?" His son nodded.

"The Parais treasure?"

"Yes, they have been looting throughout the war. They will ship it to Germany and keep it for themselves. They are robbers, Phillipe. Remember that always, they're thieves and wicked men."

"What can we do to stop them, Papa?" Phillipe was sure his father would be able to do something. How could he let all those priceless antiques and paintings fall into their hands? The jewellery, the glass, the silver?

His father was looking at him.

"Yes, Phillipe, I don't want to lose it either! And I'm going to try and do something about it. The Parais treasure has been in the family too long to be taken by robbers and murderers. It will belong to you after me, Phillipe. Do you believe me?" Phillipe nodded.

"Yes, Papa, but how? He said that there would be guards and we have no lorry any more, not since it was taken by the soldiers."

"I know that. No, Phillipe, you and I and someone else — "

"Who?" Phillipe cried, wondering whom they could trust.

"You saw me speaking with Henri earlier?" Now Phillipe understood, he was relieved. Henri would never give them away, never! "Yes, we can trust him. As to how — ?" The Count stared into his son's eyes. "I didn't intend to show you this for many years, Phillipe. My father did not show me until I had reached eighteen."

"Show me what?"

"You are the heir to the Parais fortune, Phillipe and at some time in the life of the heir he is told the secret."

"Secret?" the boy asked.

"Look up there." His father pointed to the magnificent painting. "Who is it?"

"Roger d'Artaigne," Phillipe said. He had always admired the painting that hung over the massive fireplace but, if he had been quite truthful, he would have admitted to himself that it frightened him a little. Its eyes followed you all about the room and besides, it was like looking at an image of yourself. Phillipe knew he looked very much like Roger even though the man had lived two hundred years earlier.

In fact, Roger seemed to be looking at them now, his dark brown pupils blazing out of the portrait. Phillipe would rather have looked at the splendid dog that accompanied his ancestor. The animal had a magnificent collar, studded with jewels, and his paws were set on the beginning of a white road, which appeared to lead into the forest of Artaigne.

"Yes, he was a clever man," the Count said, "ingenious, in fact. He saved our family during the Revolution, and he's going to save it again."

"What do you mean, Papa?"

"I mean you must never tell anyone about this, Phillipe, except your own son."

"My son?"

"Yes, when you get married." Phillipe had hardly seen his father smile that day. Now he did at the thought of little Phillipe married. The Count walked over to the big windows of the room and looked outside as if he was afraid of anyone seeing. He made sure the curtains were drawn close and then he returned to Phillipe and the fireplace. The boy's heart was beating so fast he thought it would burst.

"You must tell no-one. You must promise."

"I promise."

"*No-one but my son*. Repeat it, Phillipe."

"No-one but my son," the boy said and his lips quivered a little. Now everything really did seem like a dream.

"Now I'll show you where we'll hide the treasure from the Nazis." His father's voice was hoarse with

80

emotion. Phillipe was sweating with fear and excitement.

The Count was taking a sturdy chair and carrying it over to the fireplace.

"No time for a step ladder," was all he said as he climbed up and reached above the ornamented stone of the mantelpiece. Phillipe ran forward to hold the chair as his father struck the portrait of Roger d'Artaigne beneath the paws of that magnificent dog. Phillipe breathed in sharply as he heard the grinding and whirring — his eyes grew bigger and bigger as a great hole in the stone wall appeared as if by magic. The wooden door the stone had concealed was enormous and banded with iron.

"There," his father said, climbing down, "there you are, my son. The passage that Roger built to save the family in times of trouble. And it's going to save us now."

"Are we going through there?"

"You cannot go right through. It's a false door. The passage is under the floor. A safety device in case the door was discovered by builders or such. Come on." Phillipe watched his father shove and push against the wood so he got his shoulder to it as well. The door gave way into a small room with a flagged floor, each one emblazoned with the Parais arms cut into the stone.

"Remember now, Phillipe," his father said, "find the central flag by counting from the outer walls. Step them out, my son." It took three or four minutes for Phillipe to get the idea, but when he was standing on the central stone, his father said, "Good, now stamp hard!" He jumped with all his strength and, with a jarring noise, a corner of the room ground open, revealing a dark flight of stone stairs.

"You have found it, boy!"

"Where does it lead?" Phillipe said, taking a quick look down and retreating.

"Into the open and the forest. And look." The Count brought a torch from his pocket. "There, on the top stair." The figure of a dog was cut there.

"The dog in the picture!" Phillipe cried. "I always liked that dog, Papa."

"And so did I! And I always will!" The Count suddenly picked up Phillipe and hugged him. "Now, tonight we'll wait for Henri and then we're going to have to work very, very hard if we are going to get all our valuables stowed in Roger's passage."

"Are we going to leave them there?" Phillipe cried.

"Yes, until it's safe to fetch them out again."

"When will that be?"

"Who knows? When the war's over, I suppose, and we are safe!"

"But what about Henri knowing where the passage is? Won't he tell?"

"He won't know it's a secret passage," the Count said. "We'll leave it open just like this and stow in the stuff. We'll take down Roger's picture and put that in too. We can't leave him to the Nazis. He wouldn't like that one bit."

"And, that way, no-one will know about the dog!"

"Good, you have intelligence as well, Phillipe!" The boy was happy with the praise. "And, later on, when you're a very big boy, you and I will be able to put old Roger back where he belongs — over the fireplace."

"I will, Papa, I promise." The boy remembered that promise many years after the incident.

The next two days were spent moving the art collection and antiques into the secret way beneath the Château. They could not have managed without Henri, who was a strong and trustworthy young man.

They left the painting of Roger until last. The Count made sure that Henri was not in the room when he removed it from the wall, just in case the gamekeeper might see how the mechanism worked, but Roger d'Artaigne had been a master of his art and, when the picture came down, there was only a stone panel set innocently beneath the paws of Roger's hunting hound.

Phillipe had wondered at the size of the passage. It was as wide as any carriageway and shored up with stone like a crypt. In its walls were iron sconces which, once, had flamed with pitch torches. As his father, Henri and he had strained along with their burdens, Phillipe had imagined his ancestor hurrying along friends and family to safety.

"Is it a very long passage?" he had questioned his father.

"Yes, Phillipe. It stretches to Lange."

"Lange? The village?" Phillipe could hardly believe it.

"No, Phillipe. Lange, the Château."

"What do you mean, Papa?"

"I mean that it comes out somewhere under the Château Lange. You know that they have always been our friends — "

"Yes," Phillipe replied, doubtfully. He was thinking of Mamselle Chard. He did not feel that she was particularly friendly. There was something he did not like about her. He quite liked her twin brother though. He was a very good friend and had taken Phillipe shooting and riding many times.

"In the time of the Revolution, the Chards and Roger and our family met up in the passage and fled. However, where the passage comes up in the forest, I don't know. That part is blocked off now." Phillipe's heart turned in his chest. Somehow he had imagined he, Papa and Henri would be able to get away from the Nazis through the passage and out into the forest like Roger had. When he said this to his father, the Count smiled.

"Those days are over, Phillipe. Escape isn't that easy now." Those were words that Phillipe never forgot.

The night before the fourth day was up, they had a visitor. Mamselle Chard.

The Count seemed very glad to see her, but Phillipe hung back when she kissed him. She didn't seem to notice that but she certainly noticed the absence of the treasures. She looked at his father, raised her eyebrows questioningly but said nothing. At least, Phillipe heard her say nothing but he was told to go to bed fairly soon after.

The last he saw of the Countess Chard for many years was she and his father embracing in a goodbye under the archway of the Château. As Phillipe looked from his vantage point on the stairs he was wondering if his father had told her about the passage.

But then he remembered that only a male heir was to know and thought that her brother must be the only one to know of the other end of the passage at the Château Lange. But, then, afterwards he wondered what the family did about twins. He fell asleep still trying to puzzle it out.

On the morning of the fourth day, his father came to his bedroom early. Phillipe noticed with a shock that Papa was wearing the dress uniform that he had worn for ceremonial occasions before the war. He was going to ask why but he just didn't. He was too afraid.

His father sat by the bed and held his hand. Phillipe always remembered his last words.

"Phillipe, today someone is coming to take you away from here."

"Take me away. I won't go! I'm staying with you, Papa."

"No, you cannot. You are the only Parais left and you are precious. The Nazis want to take you as much as they wanted to take the treasure. They will take neither. Père Cathé will come for you."

"But how shall I get away with him? And what will you do?"

"Leave that to him. The priest is a clever man." Phillipe knew what that meant. Père Cathé hated the Germans and it was whispered he was one of the Resistance. There was nothing Phillipe could do that morning when his father woke him at dawn, except to go with Père Cathé, who arrived dressed in dungarees and looking more like a farm hand than a priest.

He had ridden from Lange on a

bicycle, carrying a churn of milk in the small trailer he was pulling behind. He had been challenged at the gates and his little trailer had been examined by the guards. When they had found nothing, they had let the priest through.

Phillipe watched his father and the priest tip the milk away into the kitchen sink and, soon after that, Phillipe was leaving his home for the last time, curled up inside the churn, which had a removable neck so that a small boy could squeeze himself inside.

Phillipe never saw his father, the Comte de Parais, again . . .

5

MARCEL DE PARAIS stopped his story and Stella brought her mind back to the present. She had been so absorbed by the tale that she was hoping that the young man must go on and tell her the rest. He couldn't stop now. His face was pale and what he had been saying must have been an ordeal.

"Please, Marcel, what happened to your father? Did he get away? He must have! What happened to your grandfather when the Nazis found the treasure had disappeared?" Stella knew she was prying but she also realised she had to know the truth about the young professor's masquerade.

"All right, Stella, I'll tell you. When the Commandant came back with the soldiers and found the Parais treasure had disappeared, he questioned my grandfather under torture and, when they could get nothing from him, he had him shot. They left him hanging from the banisters of the great staircase and then they set fire to the Château d'Artaigne."

"How terrible. Oh, I'm sorry! And your father?"

"Père Cathé hid him for quite a time and, when he judged it safe, found a place for Phillipe with some patriots and friends in a village not far from St Ayr. That is where he finally grew up and married some years later. I was born in that village. But, Stella, my family wasn't the only one to suffer then. Think of Lange."

"I am. That was terrible too."

"They thought that Count Chard had a hand in my disappearance as the family was so friendly with ours. They questioned the Count — he was as much a hero as my grandfather. They knew that he ran the local resistance and they were ready to shoot him, his wife, and his daughter, Céline, just as readily as they shot my father.

"Anyway, when the Nazis finally threatened to burn down the Château at Lange as well, the Countess betrayed her family and told the Nazis about the Resistance.

"Her own brother, his wife, and many villagers died."

"The Nazis let Céline go?"

"Yes, because the Countess had collaborated and Père Cathé pleaded for the baby's life!

"He was a brave man," Marcel said simply. "Without his help my father would not have survived and we would not be having this conversation. He has also been the means of me being able to keep in touch with Céline Chard."

"Please tell me the rest now, Marcel," Stella said, looking at her watch. They had been talking for over an hour and she was afraid that someone would tell the Countess she was still in the Château grounds.

"My father told me nothing of the

story nor the existence of the Parais treasure until I was ready to take my doctorate at St Ayr. He was very proud of my academic progress and he wanted me to know that I could take up my professorship without worrying about money.

"He was confident that he would be able to find the treasure still in Roger's passage. He was also near to being able to claim back the lands of Artaigne after some legal dispute. In fact, everything was going very well until — "

"Until what?"

"Until he died." The words were flat.

"Oh, Marcel, I'm sorry. And you still don't know where the passage is."

"You are going too fast as usual, Stella. That isn't quite right. I do know where the passage is."

"Well, then?" Stella didn't understand.

"My father and I visited the Artaigne grounds and the ruins of the Château

93

about two years ago. Do you know, Stella, I have been approached by a building firm who want to rebuild the place and make it into flats!" He shrugged and shook his head. "I refused, of course."

"Tell me about when you went there."

"This is the worst part of the story — for me anyway." He breathed in. "The grounds are still quite lovely although they are choked with weeds and foliage and everything looks so unkempt. Everything is so run down I couldn't believe it. That's why I need the treasure — "

"I understand. Of course, I do. I'd feel the same — " She broke off because he was looking approvingly at her. An unfamiliar warmth was spreading through her and Stella knew her instincts about him had been correct. He was no crook; she was sure that everything he was telling her was perfectly true.

"Thank you, Stella, for trusting me,"

he said. "I need someone to believe in what I'm doing.

"Anyway, my father and I picked and hacked our way through what seemed like mountains of brambles and bushes. It was the time for berries and some of the creepers had climbed up the ruined walls and were hanging like vines. It actually took some hours to get our bearings.

"My father was only young, you know, when he left and he could hardly remember where any of the rooms had been. It was really funny. He kept pointing out things and saying, 'Look, that's where the pig sty used to be!' It was very strange." Marcel's voice was soft as he spoke about his father; Stella could see he had loved him a lot.

"He was very tired and out of breath. I should have noticed but I was too busy looking for the passage entrance.

"How we scraped away the soil in that area; it was extremely hard work, but I was using the spade. He wasn't very strong. I knew he'd been ill and my mother had said I had to do all the donkey work. She didn't want us to go. She agreed because she could do little else.

"Anyway, we found the floor of what remained of the room. It took us a whole six hours to clear it. Then we had to find the right stone."

"And did you?" Stella could hardly contain herself.

"Yes. The mechanism to Roger's passage was still in working order. The steps were revealed most perfectly.

"My father and I took torches and tackle and entered the passage. The treasure had been stored a good way inside and my father had actually counted the sconces which used to hold the torches. He was sure that there were fifty or so before the treasure would be revealed. And then — "

"Yes?" Stella could hardly breathe.

"We came to a dead end. The tunnel had been bricked up. It would have taken an explosion to move the obstruction. We had no explosives, no expertise; we knew the dangers. The tunnel might have collapsed with us in it."

"But how could it have happened? Who could have done it?"

"There was no living person who could have known about the passage, except the gamekeeper. He died during the war and he didn't know the secret of opening the floor. No, there is only one explanation. The passage must have been bricked up by people coming through from the other end."

"You mean the Lange end?"

"Exactly." Marcel took off his glasses and looked her straight in the eyes. "As I said that is the only explanation. Someone from the Château Lange had the passage bricked up and removed the treasure."

"Yet the only person who should have known would have been the Comte de Chard?"

"Yes and he was shot. Céline was too young and, also, there has been no precedent for telling a female member of the family, heir or not."

"So it had to be the Countess — ?" Marcel nodded.

"Exactly. There was no-one else. When her brother died she was heir."

"He wouldn't have told her, would he? He was shot because of her collaboration. He couldn't have told her then."

"Perhaps she had known before. Because they were twins, perhaps the old Count had told both of them? I am guessing, Stella, I keep on guessing. But remember my father saw her visit my grandfather. She must have found out that the treasures were in the passage for safe keeping and decided to keep them for herself."

"Oh, no, how could she?"

"Quite easily, Stella. Look what she did to her own brother!"

"Do you think it was the Nazis? Do you think they found the passage?"

"That I do not know. I pray not. But I have to find the Lange entrance,

Stella. As much as Céline does."

"Does Céline know all this?" Stella asked.

"Céline knows everything. She knows of the Parais treasure but what she fears most of all is that her aunt is going to disinherit her. If she can find the passage, then she will have a very strong lever to make the old girl pay for her sins."

"Blackmail, really, I suppose, but the Countess deserves it!"

"I agree, Stella. I have never advocated an eye for an eye but, in this case, I think justice would be the right word. That was a day I will never forget. Twenty four hours after we discovered the passage had been blocked, my father was dead.

"He had a massive coronary brought on by the shock. Of course, he had been suffering from angina and he didn't want me to know."

"I'm so sorry, Marcel," Stella said, putting out her hand. He took hers and held it.

"He did recover consciousness before he died and I promised him that I would find the Parais treasure. I am sure he was satisfied. He knew I could be relied upon to keep my word.

"A month or so after his death I decided to start making all the inquiries I could. I got in touch with Père Cathé again and he helped us to get together. But, unfortunately, things have started to go wrong. I have found, sadly, that I cannot trust Céline. I'm afraid she may have a tendency to greed as well. I have been watching her most carefully and I think she's going to try and find Roger's treasure and keep some of it for herself."

"But that's terrible," Stella cried, "after all you have been through!"

"But it's also human nature," Marcel said. "One has to fight for what one wants. Céline has always known that. Coupled with hatred, it's a very potent mixture."

"And the man she was talking

to — when you pulled me into the bushes?"

"I don't know who he is. But Père Cathé and I have been trying to get to the bottom of things," he explained.

"Then you — "

"Walked into it all that night at the church hall! I'm sorry."

"Don't be," he said unexpectedly. "I'm fairly glad you did, because now you'll be able to help too."

"Will I?" Stella asked. Her heart was beating fast.

"At first I thought that there was no chance you would believe the story, but I see I was wrong. I'm sure you would like to see the final proof of my identity, wouldn't you, Stella?" Marcel was putting his hand inside his heavy cotton jacket. He withdrew an expensive-looking wallet. He opened it and took out a card. He handed it to her.

Stella looked at the face staring at her from the passport-sized photograph. It was his formal identity card bearing the name, 'Marcel de Parais', his address in St Ayr and his profession. She handed it back to him.

"Thank you, but I didn't really need to see it, Marcel. I believed you."

"I just wanted you to be sure." Stella was amazed by how pleasant he could be; how different from that first night in the hall at the back of the church. She had thought he was arrogant then, now she knew he wasn't at all, that he had only been protecting his interests.

"How can I help?" she asked simply.

"Before I tell you I want to say how grateful I am that you wish to be part of this hunt for my inheritance. I know that sounds impossibly — "

"Romantic?" They laughed so easily that she almost forgot the seriousness of the situation.

Suddenly Marcel was very close to her.

"It could be dangerous, Stella. I have to tell you that. I'll understand if you refuse."

"Oh, no, I want to help you and

Père Cathé. I'm not afraid; well, I don't think I am!" He was smiling at her honesty and, all the time, she was watching that smile sweeten the corners of his strong mouth. Stella suddenly realised that she was attracted to Marcel more than to any man she had ever met. Her senses were telling her that was why she was taking the risk. She began wondering if he felt anything like that about her.

"I'm not asking you to do much, Stella, only that you deliver a message to Père Cathé." She nodded and he took a gold ballpoint and a small notepad from his pocket. He scribbled on the paper very quickly.

"Here, read it."

Stella stared at the words in horror.

'*If you haven't heard from me by morning, contact the police and tell them everything. Our lives may depend on it. M. de P.*'

"It's that dangerous?"

"I hope not, but I have to cover myself. Who knows? Yet one thing

I'm sure of. We shall find that passage tonight and, with luck, the treasure!"

"You'll be careful?"

"I will. Don't be afraid. It's sweet of you to think of me." To her horror, she realised she was blushing. She took the note and pushed it into her pocket. In a moment, he was resting his hand on her arm once more. Then, suddenly, he caught her to him and kissed her lightly on the cheek. As he did so she closed her eyes for one tiny moment allowing a thrill to pass through her. Then he let her go.

"Au revoir, Marcel," she said, pausing at the door of the little summer-house. Suddenly, she turned. "When will I see you again, Professor?"

"I'll come and visit you at Catherine's, I promise, and tell you what has happened."

"But how will you get out of the grounds?"

"The way I got in — through a small door in the wall. I can thank Père Cathé for that. He has the usual access

104

accorded to the pastor of the village. He keeps the key hidden amongst the stones." Stella remembered that she'd seen the old priest trying the arched door in the wall. Now she knew what he had been doing!

She suddenly found that she was thinking of the priest with affection instead of dislike. She realised how easy it was to take things at their face value instead of knowing the facts. Why, Père Cathé was a hero, almost.

Marcel was standing at the summer-house door as she walked down the path. She kept the picture of him in her mind. His tall, well-muscled frame, dark brown hair and eyes, expensive clothes, open-necked shirt revealing a powerful neck.

Yes, Marcel de Parais was decidedly attractive. Exciting, handsome and intelligent — the kind of man she had been always hoping she would meet and fall in love with.

Stella couldn't imagine why she was beginning to think in this way.

An hour ago she had been terrified of him; several days before she had dismissed him as arrogant and possibly a con-man. She knew she herself was behaving in a most uncharacteristic fashion and began wondering what was the matter with her.

★ ★ ★

As Marcel watched Stella Foster hurry down the path beside the lake he had several things on his mind. He certainly had no time or desire to brood on how he felt about the English girl, who had strayed quite innocently into his life.

But he couldn't get her out of his thoughts, a new experience for him. He came into contact with so many women at the university and knew several who had tried to get close to him. But he always seemed so preoccupied that he hardly had time for love. Marcel suddenly recognised he had considered the word several times in connection with Stella.

She was certainly attractive and intelligent but, he realised, there was something else between them. An easiness that comes only when a man and woman can be frank with one another, can even share the smallest thing and derive enjoyment from it.

Marcel was amazed at himself for telling her the whole story of his background. He had never done such a thing before. Then he reminded himself that he had had to because, otherwise, they would have been discovered by Céline and her accomplice. He had needed to confide in her and that was certainly a new feeling for Marcel. He usually relied on no-one except himself. Now he had asked for this girl's help and had sent her to deliver a message for Père Cathé.

The old priest would be surprised. He had told Marcel that he should not disclose anything to anyone in case they were discovered. What would he think of this new development?

Suddenly Marcel didn't care what

Père Cathé thought. Stella was involved now and Marcel realised he was glad it was only on the sidelines.

He considered what would happen when he did find the treasure. It would bring so much undesirable publicity. You couldn't keep quiet news of a priceless treasure discovered after fifty years hidden away.

Marcel didn't want the tabloids to hear. What would it to do to Céline, Père Cathé — and now Stella? Still, he had to find the treasure for his own sake and his father's and rebuild the Château d'Artaigne. He owed that to his ancestors.

The matter had certainly given Marcel a few sleepless nights and, as a rule, he slept well. He looked round the summer-house and discovered he felt tired. Marcel kept himself in good shape and rarely felt like that. He wished that the whole matter could be over quickly — as it would be tonight.

He glanced at his watch. He had

covered himself by sending the message by Stella. Naturally, Père Cathé had wanted to be in at the end, but Marcel was not going to have an old man, friend or not, hampering him in any way. Marcel had been slipping in and out of the gate in the wall for a few days now and Céline had been spiriting him down into the cellars. Marcel had already made a start at looking for the door to the passage.

He was convinced it would work on the same principle as the opening on the Artaigne side and the maps of the cellars had been very helpful. He was also very sure he would find another pavement, with the Lange arms this time.

He, Père Cathé and Céline had worked it all out with the knowledge the three of them possessed. They had assessed the direction and the possibilities and Marcel was sure he was right. The arms of Lange contained the emblem of a stag and Marcel put two and two together.

The oldest map showed a part of the cellar was called 'The Stag's Leap' — in fact, there was a wine named after it. He reasoned he was looking for the stag and he was sure he had found the spot. Behind a very ancient row of barrels they had discovered the emblem cut in the stone. Céline had stared at it without understanding and Marcel, wary of her, had not given the slightest clue as to how it could help them find the passage.

He was due to meet Céline in an hour to discuss the coming night's visit to the cellars. Marcel was sure that this time he would find out what had happened to the Parais inheritance.

As he walked by the lake under the cover of the sweet-smelling bushes he was thinking, strangely, not of Artaigne and Roger, but of the English girl, Stella Foster and wondering if she had managed to deliver the message to Père Cathé.

When she had lost sight of Marcel, Stella began thinking very carefully. She believed the story, however amazing it seemed to be. She acknowledged the attraction she felt for Marcel de Parais and she decided that, besides carrying this message, she wanted to see the whole thing through.

She found herself planning a later return to the Château Lange to help Marcel further.

He had mentioned danger. She didn't exactly know what he meant. Of course, she had felt threatened and frightened when he had grabbed her so that Céline and the mysterious man would not find her, but she couldn't see how they could hurt her.

After all, Marcel was only looking for what belonged to him and he could prove it. And why shouldn't she help him?

She suddenly stopped walking and found herself on the fringe of the aviaries. She really wanted to be with the man. He had become so important to her. Why? She stood stupidly asking herself questions she didn't want to answer.

The aviaries were long, mellow buildings covered in creepers and a profusion of blossoms and butterflies. They had tiled roofs and, against each wall, were wire netting cages so the birds could fly about almost as if they had true freedom. It was ironic that she was standing by a building where the pretty lovebirds were swooping in pairs. She turned away and towards another building which housed a variety of screaming parakeets.

They were too much to listen to, so she walked through and on in the direction of the gatehouse, the bulk of the Château Lange to her left.

Stella suddenly wondered if Céline had been looking for her. She had been in the gardens for ages. She sauntered around, feigning interest.

Stella stopped to look at the fountain which fed the lake. It was so beautiful. A Triton, made of green bronze, was leaping high in the air and water was pouring from his mouth and horn. The water then fed the four stags which stood drinking, their smooth bronze mouths destined to taste that water for ever.

Stella watched the water run down and down a series of steps and pools towards the lake from where she had just come. The Château Lange was a beautiful place on that summer afternoon. She closed her eyes just to calm herself and to try to forget, for a moment, Marcel de Parais and the strange story he had told.

Behind the dull red of her eyelids she could feel the sun on her face. She put up her hand and pulled off the bandeau, letting her hair free. She tossed it back and her eyes suddenly sprang open as she felt a hand on her shoulder. She jumped and saw Céline Chard.

"Are you still here, Miss Foster?" she asked rudely.

"Oh, I'm so sorry, Mamselle Chard-Montaigne. It's been such a lovely day, the weather and all, and I spent so much time in the aviaries and by the lake — " Stella was sure that Céline's eyes showed a flicker of alarm but she immediately regained her composure.

"The birds are wonderful. As for the fountain — well, what can I say?

"I am sorry," she repeated, "but I didn't know that you were waiting for me to leave. It took such a long time to walk round — "

"I don't mind, Miss Foster," Céline replied, "but my aunt is not at all keen on visitors. As you know she is something of a recluse. She values her privacy enormously."

"But she did say I could see everything," Stella insisted, hoping that her apparent naivety would pay off.

"That's true — and I'm sure, in this case, she wouldn't mind. But, now, I do think it would be wise if you — "

"Left," Stella finished. "Of course, and I've had a wonderful time. I will treasure it." The word slipped out so easily, Stella thought Céline would surely notice, but she didn't seem to. "Thank you so much and goodbye."

Céline was following her. She's probably making sure I get out, Stella thought as she made for the gatehouse. They were soon standing under the arch. The older woman looked at Stella.

"You came up by car, Miss Foster?"

"No, only half the way. My friend, Catherine, dropped me off. I like walking. That way I can see the countryside."

"I could ask Johann to drive you down."

"Goodness me, no thank you," Stella replied. It was the last thing she wanted; she was determined to examine the gate in the wall on the way down.

"It'd be no trouble," Céline persisted. Stella knew she was making sure that Stella got away — and fast!

"No, I prefer walking," Stella insisted firmly.

"Very well then." Stella held out her hand.

"Goodbye, Mamselle Chard-Mont-aigne, I've had the most entertaining day and I've learned so much. Please thank your aunt again for me."

"I will," Céline Chard said. Stella hoped the thank you hadn't been too theatrical, but she'd never played a part like this before.

"Goodbye, Miss Foster. I'll certainly express your thanks. Madame Blois," she called, then walked away without looking over her shoulder. Stella stood at the gate, waiting to be let out.

Madame Blois had changed into an even smarter dress and discarded her espadrilles for neat court shoes. She chattered on as she escorted Stella through the gates of the Château Lange.

"Thank you so much, madame," Stella said, glancing up at the leaded windows of the gatehouse, wondering how much of the road Madame Blois could see from her rooms upstairs. Then Madame Blois waved her goodbye and Stella was breathing a sigh of relief as she disappeared.

Thank goodness I'm out, she thought. Now to find out how to get in again. Looking behind her furtively, Stella walked down the hill. With one final glance over her shoulder, she said a tiny prayer and slipped inside the archway of the gate in the wall.

"Now where's the key?" she said under her breath. "He said something about stones. This must be it." She sifted through the pile of stones beside the step and discovered the key.

She had never done anything like this before; the idea of entering someone's house and grounds was an entirely alien thing. The thought made her tremble. Then she remembered the earnest, pleading face when Marcel de Parais had said he needed her help, wanted her to believe him.

She didn't bother to try the key in the lock. She was sure that it would fit and equally sure that it would be there when she needed it that evening. She replaced it carefully and came out into the full sunshine of the road, wiping her hands down the side of her already muddied skirt. She wondered suddenly if Céline Chard had noticed how grubby she looked. Well, she couldn't suspect Stella more than she did already.

★ ★ ★

She was quite tired when she reached the gates of St Michel. She had to deliver the message straight away. Stella knew there was no time to return to Catherine's to change.

Under the watchful eyes of the leering gargoyles Stella walked round the church towards the presbytery, which was beyond the hall. The latter had a dead and silent air and its door had a heavy lock upon it.

The priest's house looked most forbidding even in the afternoon sun. Père Cathé didn't seem to be in.

She knocked sharply on the door.

Their was an air of shabbiness about the entrance. The stone step was well-worn and there were one or two crusts thrown hurriedly on the side garden, presumably to feed the birds. There was also a saucer for a cat with half-dried milk left upon its surface and a small earthenware bowl.

There was no reply. Stella shifted about from one leg to the other. She was much more tired than she'd thought, but she had walked a long way and been through a lot. She was also hungry.

Still, she decided to look through the window, which was fairly wide though somewhat high. Stella wasn't that tall and it meant scrambling through some creepers and standing on tiptoe.

It was as she would have expected. It was the home of a bachelor and an ascetic. A large room with all its walls lined with bookcases. A scholar's room, in fact. There were two comfortable-looking old armchairs with lace antimascassars and an equally ancient settee, strewn with papers. Piled beside the chairs were newspapers.

Over the fireplace hung a gloomy oil painting depicting a religious scene and the mantleshelf was crammed with everything from a razor to a pile of coins. Hanging behind the door was a black coat but, suddenly, Stella noticed another garment thrown carelessly over the arm of one chair.

It was an expensive jacket, an incongruous contrast to the rest of the shabby room. It most certainly was Marcel's. He was clearly living here with Père Cathé. Also, there were two coffee mugs placed on a three-legged table.

Stella decided she would have to post the letter under his door — she couldn't see a letter box anywhere.

She withdrew the note and pushed it carefully under, using the slight well of the worn step to help her. It was at that moment the cat turned up. He was evidently hoping his master had returned. Stella stroked him.

"Don't forget, Puss, make sure he sees it!" She grinned at her own foolishness and straightened. She hoped so much that he would or everything could go wrong.

6

IT was always difficult meeting Céline in the Château grounds. Marcel had to make sure that none of the staff saw him and that the Countess was safely out of the way. The greatest danger came from Johann, who was to be found in all kinds of places. Johann had household affairs under constant surveillance and was really the one who mattered in the servants' eyes.

They resented taking orders from a mistress whom they despised, but they respected Johann. He wasn't a full German. He had been born in Lange and no-one seemed to care that his father had been one of the Nazis. Most of the Countess's servants were young enough to know very little about the war and those who knew didn't seem to care.

Marcel had wondered sometimes if Johann knew about the existence of the treasure. He was an astute man and had not always worked for the Countess. Céline said that he had been something quite big in the Civil Service but had become fed up with his desk job and returned to his birthplace.

Naturally, Marcel knew about Johann's relationship with Catherine. His suspicions had been aroused when Stella, who was staying with Catherine, had walked in on the meeting in the church hall.

It had been just too much of a coincidence. It had seemed even stranger that Johann had been able to get Stella into the Château.

However, after speaking to Stella at the lake, it was clear she was an innocent in the whole matter. Indeed, it was clear it was Céline who was up to something. Marcel couldn't help but wonder about the identity of the man Céline had met that afternoon.

Whoever he was, he, too, had to be skulking somewhere nearby waiting for nightfall to search for the passage — and the treasure.

As Marcel waited in the shelter of a high wall, he tried to work out the best way to play this final meeting with Céline, now he knew she was double-crossing him.

Suddenly he heard feet approaching along the gravel path. If it was Céline, it was uncharacteristic — she was never on time. It was, though — surely another confirmation of her guilt. He bit his lip, then stepped out of the shadows to confront her.

She jumped.

"Good Heavens, Marcel, what a fright you gave me! Come out of sight. You don't want anyone to see us from the house, do you?" Céline grasped his arm and Marcel let her lead him into the cover of the trees.

"You mean Johann, I suppose, or could you mean Miss Foster?" He caught the momentary flicker of surprise on her face. "This was the day she was due, wasn't it? Very awkward."

"She's been and gone, Marcel," Céline replied. "I saw her off the premises myself."

"That's what I like to hear," he said, only thankful to learn that nothing had gone wrong.

"I can't stand the girl myself. Far too inquisitive!"

"You don't have to worry about her now, Céline," he remarked casually. "We can forget her. There's no way that she could know anything about anything. She's just a student."

Céline nodded but Marcel knew she wasn't really concentrating. Marcel would have liked to have known what was going on in her head. She was very nervous, an occasional tic showed in her cheek and she put up a hand to disguise it. She also avoided eye contact and kept looking down at the borders and her feet.

"Have you been inside the grounds long, Marcel? It is dangerous, you know. If my aunt saw you — "

"She wouldn't recognise me," he replied.

"She might not, but she would certainly call the police."

"And Johann?"

"Who knows what he would do. He's too shrewd for words!

"But why are we talking about them? We're so near now. I'm sure you've worked out where the passage is. I wish you'd tell me. I can't wait to find the treasure." She glanced at him, her eyes not ducking his this time. "Marcel, you know why, don't you? I can't wait to get even with my aunt after all this time."

"Revenge will do you no good, Céline," he said. It sounded sanctimonious, but it was a fact. Hate was eating her up.

"How can you say that? You can't understand how I feel. Remember, I lost both my parents!"

"I know. But I've lost a lot as well. If it hadn't been for what the Countess did, my father would be alive and, maybe, even my grandfather."

"So why don't you care as much as me?"

"I do, but I also care about justice. If she has taken what's mine, I'll make her pay, but within the law," he said. "If you don't, you'll end up like her, despising yourself."

"You are holy today, Marcel," she said bitterly. "You must have been talking to Père Cathé. Where is he, anyway?"

"I've told him not to come tonight. We don't need him. He's done enough and he can't be seen to be involved in this. He's a man of the Church."

"But can we manage alone?" Céline asked. "I'm not very strong."

"My dear Céline," he replied, "you don't think that you and I are going to move the treasure if we find it? If we do, we're going to the police."

"Are we?" she said.

"You know we are. We've discussed it already."

"I wish you'd tell me where you

think the passage is," she interposed, avoiding the point.

"You'll see it when I find it," Marcel replied. "Now — let's go over the plan again. We won't start until the Countess is in bed. It's your task to make sure she goes as early as possible and let me know when she does."

"She'll probably be awkward," Céline said.

"No, she's a creature of habit. Tonight, she plays bridge with Madame Blois. You know the game tires them both. That, coupled with wine — "

"Are you suggesting I get her drunk?" Céline asked. "That wouldn't be easy."

"No, I just expect you to be nice to her, that's all. If you are, it will annoy her so much she'll call a halt to the game and go up anyway."

"Oh, you're far too clever, Marcel," Céline told him spitefully. "All right, I'll do my best to be nice to her, as nice as possible — and she'll hate it. With luck, she'll watch television in her room and won't hear any noise."

"What makes you think there'll be any?"

"Well, you'll have to knock the wall down, won't you?" Céline was fishing.

"Most probably," Marcel replied, smiling. He was as good at the game as she.

"How will I let you know she's gone up?" Céline asked. There were two spots of red on her cheeks and she was tracing the line of her lips with her tongue. She looked extremely guilty.

"Go along to your room and open your bedroom window. I'll be waiting in the shrubbery. Then come down and let me in."

"And the servants?"

"Really, Céline, don't tell me you've never let a man come up to your room at night!" Her face flared. She turned away from him.

"I'll do what you say." Then she turned back. "You're sure you'll find it tonight?"

"I shall," Marcel said. "I didn't get this far not to." He saw her look of relief. It wasn't any sense of mischief that prompted his last words to Céline Chard, but rather a veiled warning. "Don't forget, Céline, that I'm a Parais and all of us have been known for our intelligence."

"Don't you mean your arrogance, Parais?" she replied, walking off. Then she stopped. "Don't worry. I'll get you in."

After Marcel had withdrawn to the spot he was hiding in, he opened the box of rolls and cheese that Père Cathé had packed for him that morning. He drank none of the wine as he was afraid that it might dull his reactions. Looking at his watch again, he settled down to get some rest before he began one of the most important excavations in his life . . .

If Stella hadn't been so preoccupied with her plans for the night, she would have been quite content to go on sampling each piquant course that Catherine placed before her and Johann.

Stella stared at the wafer-thin slices of ham arranged with the kind of salad a good French cook makes completely irresistible.

"What's the matter, Stella? You don't seem to have much appetite this evening." Catherine sat down opposite Johann, who smiled at her, then at Stella.

"I'm just tired from my day out."

"The Château's a big place," Johann remarked. "I can vouch for that. The miles I've walked through those grounds! Did you see the summer-house?"

Stella glanced at him quickly, thinking for a moment that he might be trying to find out about her meeting earlier that day with Marcel. But she dismissed the thought. She was just getting paranoid about the whole thing, suspecting everybody she came in contact with. Johann couldn't possibly have anything to do with the Parais inheritance!

"Oh, yes, I did see the summer-house," she replied. "It's absolutely lovely, isn't it? And in such a wonderful position by the lake. Do you go there sometimes, Johann?"

"Practically every day." Johann smiled. Stella's heart jumped. Had he seen her? "But not today because I was extra busy. As the Countess had a guest, she left me to do all her work."

"I'm sorry, Johann," Stella said, relieved.

"No, it doesn't matter at all. I can stand being inside for a day. Anyway, I had tonight to look forward to," he added gallantly. The couple smiled at each other and once again Stella felt that she was in the way.

Stella thought how well-suited they were as they sat opposite each other on the small terrace, sipping red wine. Johann's fair hair was silvery in the moonlight and his eyes were bright as he listened to Catherine's sophisticated conversation.

He was witty, too, and Catherine

laughed a great deal, evidently enjoying his company. Stella thought Catherine looked very young. Her face was barely lined and her throat still young and supple. About her neck was a single string of pearls, the cool whiteness of which was accentuated by the midnight blue chiffon dress.

Johann stretched out a hand too and took hers across the table. It was a most romantic gesture. Stella leaned back in her chair and concentrated on the noises of the night, going over her future escapade so as not to make any mistakes.

"Are you sure you're all right, Stella? You don't seem yourself this evening," Catherine remarked suddenly.

"Don't I? Oh, I'm sorry if I'm being rude. I was just thinking how beautiful everything is."

"Thank you," Catherine replied. "Yes, I love Lange, too. What would I do if I had to leave all this?" She gestured towards the garden, which was sleeping under the cover of warm night.

"Leave?" Stella repeated. "You're not thinking of it surely?" They smiled at her anxious looks.

"No, it was just my way of speaking," Catherine said. "I have had enough of big cities, but Johann — " She broke off.

"Are you moving, then?" Stella directed her question to him. He shrugged.

"Maybe. But I'm not sure."

"Don't you — " Now it was Stella's turn to break off. She was thinking how impolite it would be to pry into the couple's affairs.

"Please carry on, Stella," Johann replied. "Honestly, you may say anything you wish. I won't be offended."

"Don't you like working at the Château?" Stella hadn't meant the question to be so pointed.

"I do, but there are other things that I must do with my life. Catherine knows that."

"Johann used to work in Paris, too," Catherine explained. "He finds Lange a bit of a backwater sometimes."

"Yet you were born here?" Stella said.

"That's probably why," he said. "In the beginning it was an experiment."

"And now?" Stella asked.

"The experiment may be coming to an end. It all depends," Johann replied, looking at Catherine, who nodded.

Stella laid her fork aside. She couldn't go on prying into their affairs.

"Well, I do hope everything goes well for you, Johann. It's always difficult making tough decisions. I'm sorry, Catherine, but I've finished. As always, it was a wonderful meal. I'm sure I'll never be able to cook like that."

"It all depends on whom one's cooking for," Catherine replied wisely.

Suddenly, Stella had a vision of her seated opposite Marcel de Parais, holding his hand, drinking red wine.

"I agree," she said, "but I'll have to wait to find out." Johann laughed and nodded.

"Too right, Stella, and I'm sure that day won't be too far off. Catherine, this English friend of yours is quite enchanting." Suddenly, Stella couldn't wait to get on with what she had been planning.

"Will you forgive me?" she said to her two companions. "I am very tired."

"Of course," Catherine said. "Do you want me to wake you in the morning?"

"No, no, I'll be fine. I've nothing very important planned for tomorrow." As she rose from the table, Johann got to his feet.

"Goodnight, Stella," he said. He turned to Catherine. "The meal was fantastic as always. I am going to have to go soon, too, as I told you earlier. Duty calls." He looked serious then and Stella realised that Catherine did not seem the least put out by his early departure. It was then that Stella envied her friend the easy relationship the pair enjoyed. Half an hour or so after Stella had retired to her room, she heard Johann saying goodbye. Stella realised that knowing Johann was at the Château Lange did not diminish her sudden apprehension.

7

INSTEAD of getting into bed, Stella was planning what she should take with her. She dressed herself in the most practical clothes she had — jeans, shirt and sweater. She pulled on her trainers, knowing they were substantial, comfortable and, above all, noiseless. She had no idea of anything she might need for this adventure so she put a screwdriver and a small torch in her pockets. She also wrote down the phone number of the local gendarmerie — just in case.

She added her house key to the list. She would have looked a fool if she eventually crept back to Catherine's only to have to stay out in the garden all night. Then, checking her watch by the digital clock radio, she went out, quietly closing the bedroom door behind her. Getting out of the house was no problem as Catherine was seated watching television in the big lounge.

Once in the cobbled street she stood for a moment under one of the street lights and looked up at the few lights of the Château Lange, high on its crag. She hoped she wouldn't be too tired after her strenuous trek earlier in the day. She stared across to the outline of the church spire silhouetted against the light night sky. There were no lights up there. Stella hoped so much that Père Cathé had received her note. She began to walk in the direction of the Château, keeping to the inner side of the pavement and, when that ceased, to the grass verge and the protecting bushes and railings.

It was an eerie walk. Once or twice she looked across and down the hill towards the village. Its friendly and familiar lights were receding and the noises of the town seemed to float up, suspended in the night air.

She was glad she had brought her torch but was reluctant to use it. However, when she reached the archway in the wall and was sure she couldn't be seen from the Château, she pointed its beam at the conical pile of stones and withdrew the key. The gate in the wall creaked unmercifully when she pushed it open. Stella waited anxiously, but not a soul had heard.

She was inside the wall. But where? She had to stand for a moment to find her bearings. She blamed herself for being an idiot for not thinking about how she was going to get into the building itself.

She wondered how Marcel got in. What she would do was to keep on walking around until an opportunity arose. Perhaps someone would leave a window open? She was at a loss, realising what a hopeless criminal she would be. She also realised there was probably a sophisticated alarm system. Stella sighed. Now she had actually made it, she was behaving like a wimp. She just had to get in for her own satisfaction — and to help Marcel.

Just then a door banged, making her heart give a guilty leap. Was someone coming out or going in? Could it be Marcel? Could it be Johann? What would he say if he found Stella trespassing? It was too awful to think of. She remained where she was, conscious of her heavy breathing, which seemed so loud it must be apparent to whoever was walking outside. Then she heard a woman's voice:

"Chuck, chuck, chuck . . . !" With a dizzy sense of relief she realised it was one of the servants sent out to get the ducks into their pen for the night.

From which door had the person come? That could be the only way in for Stella. She moved in the direction of the voice assessing the direction. The maid couldn't have come far in that short time. Stella's feet suddenly felt gravel and she was acutely conscious of the scrunching noise.

She was sure someone would hear so, summoning up her courage and an extra burst of energy, she sprinted

141

across the open space of the path towards the house. She exhaled with relief at the sight of a crack of light. A heavy door had been left ajar!

Not thinking of the danger any more, Stella pressed herself close against the flowering bushes, which sprang from the Château's wall, and slipped towards the entrance.

Breathing in very deeply, she pulled at the door and was quietly inside and standing in a short stone-flagged passage. She could hear voices. Glancing behind her and praying that the maid wouldn't return yet, Stella tiptoed along until she turned a corner into another long passage.

There was an open door to her right, the light from the room throwing a shaft of brightness into the dark corridor. She could hear the sound of cutlery, cooking utensils and laugher. The garlic smell was strong. She knew she was in the area of the kitchens.

Saying a short prayer under her breath, she dodged past and on up the corridor to the foot of a flight of stairs, which she realised led to the ground floor. Suddenly, she nearly fainted with fright.

There was a humming noise and to her left, she could see a lift was coming down. In a panic, Stella sprinted up the stairs and dived behind large velvet curtains. Enveloped in their heavy dustiness she watched the man step out of the lift. It was Johann.

Stella put a hand to her mouth, praying he was going on into the kitchens. To her relief, he turned. Sweating with fear and cursing herself for ever starting the escapade, she remained where she was, trying to calm herself.

It's no good, she told herself, getting into this state. How will you ever find the cellars or Marcel if you're behaving like a scared rabbit!

The telling-off worked. She swallowed and pushed back her hair from her face. Then she peered out through the curtains. She knew where she was — not in the Great Hall, but in a smaller hall leading off it. Through there would be the master staircase she had ascended that morning with the Countess. How long ago that seemed and how much easier!

She breathed in heavily. Now for the cellars! They would, of course, be nearer to the kitchen area than the living quarters and, from what she had seen on the map that fateful night at Père Cathé's, they stretched right under the Chateau.

It was then she could hear footsteps again, this time coming up the stairs and ready to pass Stella's hiding place. It was Johann. He passed only a few centimetres from her trembling frame. She just stayed where she was, willing him to go upstairs or wherever — as long as he went. Then she heard voices.

"I'm almost ready to lock up, Miss Chard, but the maid's still getting in the ducks. Everything else is secure."

"Thank you so much, Johann," Stella

couldn't believe that the friendly voice she was hearing was Céline's. She sounded so very nice! Not haughty, just ordinary. "You get off to bed. I'll see to that door."

"Very well, Miss Chard." Johann didn't take much persuading because Stella could hear him walking off very quickly.

Then she was conscious of Céline very near to her hiding place. She appeared to be waiting. Why didn't she go away? Panic was making Stella's heart beat very fast. Soon she'd be locked in for the night. What if Marcel hadn't been telling the truth? Then reason took over. How could what he said be a lie? Didn't she take the note to Père Cathé herself asking the police to come if he wasn't out by morning?

Suddenly, Stella was beginning to hope that Céline was loitering because she was waiting to let someone else in? Like Marcel? That must be it. That's why she had offered to lock up.

After what seemed ages she sensed

Céline was on the stairs. Stella could hear her feet going down. Then she heard another female voice:

"The ducks are safe, Madam. May I go to bed now?"

"Yes, Marie. And Cook?"

"She's gone on up."

"Good! Good-night, then!"

"Good-night." The maid didn't come up the stairs and, therefore, Stella assumed the servants' quarters were on the opposite side of the kitchens, which were central. There was the sound of keys jangling — Céline must be locking the door. Stella's heart plummeted — so there was no Marcel outside. Then she heard the man's voice.

"And about time."

"You know when Marie goes out to the animals. I told you!" Céline didn't reply and Stella stood inside the drapes, stiff with fear. Céline had not let in Marcel, but the man to whom she had been talking earlier — the man by the lake.

"Henri, don't be angry. At least I did let you in!" The voice was high and pleading.

"It would have been the worse for you if you hadn't, ma chèrie!" The endearment was quite out of place. There was nothing in his tone to suggest any sweetness. "Anyway, how's he getting on?" Stella held her breath, biting her lip.

"Marcel is doing fine," Céline replied. "He's down there, stripped to the waist, doing all our work for us," she gloated.

"Great!" Henri said. "It's working out fine. Perhaps I won't be too angry after all!"

Stella clenched her hands to her sides. This was pure, wicked greed. She wasn't going to let Marcel fall into their trap. She had to find him and do something about it — when she got out of the curtains. She wanted to sneeze — the dust was really getting to her.

"What shall we do now?" Céline asked. "I have to go back down to him. I'm worn out climbing up and down those steps."

"Is your aunt in bed?"

"She's in her room. Marcel was right about that as well. She hates me so much she can't stand me being nice to her. Also it makes her smell a rat!"

"You need never be nice to her again, Céline. The old woman's going to get what she deserves at last. She's going to have to pay for what she's done to you and me!"

Stella was trying to work out what was happening. Who was Henri — and what had the Countess done to him? It must have been something of magnitude. She shivered then felt an unmistakable tickle at the back of her throat. The dust from the curtains was choking her. She prayed she could hold back the sneeze for a little longer.

She closed her eyes and concentrated. She could hear the footsteps going away across to her left. She put a hand over her nose and mouth, feeling the curtains moving with her agitation. Then she was shaking and spluttering as the sneeze got its way at last.

She waited for repercussions — but none came. A moment later she was looking through the curtains. Céline and Henri had gone and she had to find them. She had to help Marcel, let him know. But how? She was straining her ears to listen.

Below and far to the left she could hear the dull echo of footsteps. Going in the same direction, every nerve strung tight, Stella hurried after the two conspirators. When she reached the Great Hall, she glanced up at the staircase. She was safe — then she caught sight of the small arched doorway across the hall. It was slightly ajar. Feeling sure that this was the entrance to the cellars, Stella passed by a suit of armour and under two crossed swords beneath the stag-emblazoned lintel.

There, in front of her, was a deep flight of stone stairs and from below was drifting an echoing sound.

Stella took a deep breath. The idea of going down under the Château in such risky circumstances was going to take some courage and Stella knew she'd never been particularly brave. But her fears for Marcel's safety were overcoming her own. She had to warn him somehow, but however could she reach him when she didn't even know which way Céline and her accomplice had gone.

"Now for it," Stella said, half under her breath as if to convince herself and then her right trainer was on the first worn step. She was on her way down, her feet hardly making a sound. There was a hand rail, fortunately.

Stella thought of all the poor servants who had lugged up the bottles and cases of wine over the centuries. It was utterly exhausting; the cellars were deep all right. She shivered as she made her way, becoming more stealthy and cautious with every step, listening for the echoing footsteps below her.

Occasionally, there was a recess in

the wall, a kind of resting place, but Stella had no time to get her breath. Once, when she was very deep, she had passed an iron-bound, forbidding door and her imagination ran riot as she thought of mediaeval times and wondered whether it led to the dungeons.

She dismissed the fanciful thought and carried on, her breathing getting shorter with the exertion. Her eyes had become accustomed to the dimness, but now she realised the staircase was getting lighter; maybe coming to an end? Her heart was beating very fast with excitement and fear.

She imagined herself leaping off the last step and into Henri's line of vision, so she began to creep even more cautiously around the next corner and the next. She noticed that the low ceiling had been whitewashed here and there and that, sporadically, there were modern recessed electric lights. Somehow that eased her fear and she got control of her emotions.

Quite suddenly she heard a sound — a cry of surprise or triumph or both. Stella strained her ears to listen for anything else, but there was silence. Anyway, at least, she knew there was someone down there, too! She was shaking with fear — or relief.

Stella proceeded very slowly and, as she rounded another corner she caught in her breath sharply. The staircase was opening out and, in front of her, standing together in one of those strange little recesses were Céline Chard and a stocky, dark, bearded man.

Stella shrank back, pressing herself against the wall, tightening her lips and looking upwards, hoping they wouldn't look behind. She was not going to retreat; she had to find out what they were doing and warn Marcel. But she could never ever get past them.

She peeped again and saw, with horror what the man was doing. He was taking the safety catch off a revolver! Stella stifled a cry with her hand.

Henri held the gun so easily, he

seemed used to doing so. In the harsh artificial light, Céline's face was ugly and faded. She looked scared as well; she was staring at the gun, too. Stella had to strain to hear her whisper.

"We don't need that, do we, Henri? Please?" Céline suddenly caught at the man's arm but he shook off her hand impatiently and gestured for Céline to go on in front.

The two went on slowly with Stella watching. The staircase had now opened into a great cavern-like space — the beginning of the Lange cellars. There were massive stone pillars holding up a vaulted roof like the crypt of a church. All about were racks and casks, and big barrels were everywhere. Stella breathed in deeply, feeling some relief; she knew that they would give some cover.

Céline was walking on more quickly now while Henri followed, skulking in the shadows. Behind them, Stella was dodging lightly from pillar to pillar, trying to keep up without being seen.

Her fear seemed to have dissipated in the cool air of that cavern-like place. She was calm now; thinking it out. How she could get in front of Céline and the man with that horrible gun? She had no plan, but she was attempting to formulate one.

Céline was stopping. Henri was immobile like the girl behind him.

"Marcel?" Céline called. "Marcel, I'm here, where are you?" There was no reply. Céline was looking about her, shaking her head. "Where are you, Marcel? Answer me, please."

"I'm here!" The sound was faint. "To your left." Céline, Henri and Stella swivelled in the direction of the voice. It seemed to come from the wall.

"Marcel, I can't see a thing. You've found the passage, haven't you? I know you have! Where are you?" Céline's voice was louder, more urgent. She was speaking like that so Henri could hear everything.

Suddenly, there was a creaking and

scraping sound. Stella watched one of the casks moving as if by magic. Then she realised someone was shoving it from behind.

"Here I am. Come on through, then."

"You *have* found it. Oh, Marcel, I'm coming in!"

"OK." Céline was stooping. "No, just pull and I'll push. I put the barrel in place just in case anyone else disturbed us."

"Who would do that, Marcel?" Céline said and, to Stella's horror, she could see Henri's sudden smile.

What could she do to help Marcel before they did something dreadful to him? Immediately, Céline was beginning to move inwards as if she was doing a disappearing trick. As she slipped through she gave one last warning look towards her swarthy companion. He ran forward and across to the barrels; Stella gave him one moment to squeeze himself down and Stella was fast behind him.

Then next moment Stella was on her knees staring through the opening. It led into a chamber, fairly large and supported by massive pillars. The supports were arranged in a circular shape but Stella's eyes were fixed on an opening in the floor in the middle of the circle. Céline was kneeling, talking to Marcel de Parais. He was stripped to the waist and his fine physique was instantly apparent. His back and shoulders were glistening with sweat and he was pushing his thick, dark hair and arching his neck in a gesture that spoke both of excitement and exhaustion. He was holding a storm lantern.

"Oh, Marcel," Céline cried, going to embrace him. "I'm so happy for us. How did you find it?" He was regarding her closely. "Is the treasure down there?"

"I don't know," was his reply.

"What do you mean? Why don't you know?"

"You'll have to come in to have a

look. We'll have to go on along the passage. Have you a torch?" Céline nodded. "All right." Céline was inside the opening already. The two heads disappeared. In another moment, Henri was across the floor and following. Stella had to wait some agonising moments until her turn.

The shallow steps going down from the opening revealed a broad passageway and the retreating backs of Céline and Marcel. In a split second she could see Henri below her, starting to run. In the same moment, Marcel had heard the footsteps and Stella's piercing scream: *"Look out, Marcel, he's got a gun!"*
Marcel flung himself upon the man and brought him to the ground. For one moment, Stella closed her eyes as the men grappled. She opened to see them fighting desperately; then she moved further into the passage where Céline stared at her from wide and hostile eyes. Stella and the woman were facing each other then, to Stella's horror, the gun, which had been wrested from Henri's

grasp, came spinning and slithering across the floor to rest at Cèline's feet. She sprang for it and, in one moment, Stella found herself facing the blunt muzzle.

"Stop it, Marcel, or I'll kill her!" Landing one more frantic blow, Marcel rolled off the panting Henri and the two men were staring at Cèline Chard.

"For goodness sake, Stella, don't move," Marcel cried, extending his arm in warning. Henri was struggling to his feet.

"It's all right, Cèline. Move over here. Give me the gun and I'll fix both of them!" He made a movement towards Cèline but, to the amazement of the other three, Cèline turned the gun on Henri as well.

"Now," she said, "I have all of you at my mercy. I couldn't have wanted better. Move, the lot of you. Go on, get moving. The quicker we find the treasure, the sooner this whole mess will be over.

"Move! Henri, pick up the lantern!

Now!" The man did so grudgingly. "You!" she said to Stella. "Take this torch!" She rolled it towards her and Stella bent to pick it up. "Now, at least, we have light! Right, move . . . !"

8

" CÈLINE, what on earth do you think you're doing?" Marcel shouted, eyeing the gun, looking for any chance to take it from her. "This won't do you any good. You can't handle this on your own — nor the treasure — if I find it!"

"You will, Marcel. You wouldn't be here if you didn't think you could!" Suddenly Cèline was staring at Stella. The girl felt the woman's hostility buffet her. "Neither would she!" Stella was so close to Marcel she could feel the warmth of his body, see the beads of perspiration mat the dark hair on his chest. She wanted to tell him, and only him, that she was innocent of any pre-knowledge of the Parais affair; she was desperate to say she was only here to help him.

"She knows nothing," Marcel replied,

glancing at Stella sideways. The look expressed a lot, pleading with her to know if what Cèline had said was true.

She had to say something.

"He's right, I don't know anything, only what — "

"Go on," Cèline pressed.

"I heard you by the lake!" That appeared to shake Cèline.

"You heard me?"

"Yes, I did, talking to him." Stella gestured towards Henri, who was staring at Cèline with an evil look.

"Were you following me?" Cèline cried. "How did you get in here?" The gun was waving about dangerously. Marcel put in:

"Come one, Cèline, this is no time for explanations. If you want the treasure we'd better start going down this passage." Instinctively, Stella knew he was trying to save her.

"Yes, Cèline, you haven't got time to do any explaining," Henri repeated and his voice made Stella shiver. She could

161

see open hatred in his face. "Just like a Chard; all you care for is money."

They hurried on in silence. The passage was broad, and dusty, with cobwebs hanging like fabric from the ceiling — and quite, quite empty. It was also very cold and Stella wondered how Marcel was faring without even a shirt to cover him.

Cèline was pressing them on, and the wind in the passage seemed colder.

"How far, Marcel, how far?" she asked and her voice sounded more like a hiss. He shook his head. Stella realised that perhaps there would be no treasure. Perhaps the Nazis had found the treasure and shipped it all away!

It was then that Marcel suddenly grasped her arm tightly.

"Give me the torch! Quick!"

"What are you doing?" Cèline rasped from behind. "No tricks!"

"Look, look!" he shouted. "Look there — and there!" The passage was dividing; to the left another dark hole into which Marcel swung his torch.

Stella knew that tunnel led to the forest and freedom; to the right the way was blocked. This time, not by bricks and mortar, but by furniture and packing cases, trunks and boxes.

The torch that Stella had handed to Marcel was throwing eerie shadows as it ranged in between the conglomeration of obstructions in the passage.

"This is it," he said, turning firmly towards Cèline. "Here is my treasure. But how did it get on your side of the passage?"

Cèline and her prisoners stood facing each other. The storm lantern, held by Henri, made his face a grim white mask.

"I can tell you that," he said bitterly. "It came there, like every filthy thing does, brought by the mistress of Chard!"

"Who are you?" Marcel asked. "How did you get mixed up in all this? I don't know you!"

"But I know you, sir," the man replied. "I couldn't mistake the Parais face. I've seen it all my life. You made a mistake getting mixed up with her, sir, and it looks as if I did, as well. I'll tell you who I am. I'm Henri Fasson, and — "

"Shut up!" Cèline cried.

"Fasson, Fasson — not Henri Fasson?" Marcel's voice was shaking.

"His son, sir. The son of the faithful gamekeeper, who risked his life to hide your grandfather's treasure. I had the misfortune of seeing my own father butchered by the Nazis. I never forgave the Krauts, nor the Parais family for involving my father in that.

"If he'd not been so loyal he might have been alive now. They killed him and my mother. They thought he knew where the secret passage was but he couldn't find it, could he? They looked all right, but they couldn't find a thing. Your grandfather had seen to that all right."

"He did it to save your father! Can't you see that, Fasson?"

"But he made a mistake, didn't he?

164

He was an aristocrat. He believed in the nobility of the human spirit. My father never told, he let them pull out his nails — "

"No!" Stella cried.

"Shut up, all of you. Listen to me. I'm holding the gun and I'll kill you all! I've nothing to lose now I've found it," Cèline cried.

"As for you — " She turned to Henri. "You've served your purpose. Now is the time for explanations, Marcel. I met Henri Fasson in Marseilles. And do you know, it was by chance? We just happened to meet one night in a bar. The kind of thing that happens in a book.

"I thought he cared for me, but he's just a peasant! It was finding out that we had mutual knowledge of Provence, then discovering that we had met before in the war that brought us together. I was a baby, he was a little older and he had been invited to Chateau Lange once by my father and mother as a treat for the village

165

children. That was what brought us together. Imagine, a Chard sinking to an affair with someone like this!"

There were tears coming down Cèline's cheeks and Stella could see Marcel's eyes fixed on the gun.

"But we had something else in common. We found that out one night. We found our parents had both been slaughtered! So our friendship was cemented.

"He told me that he knew about the passage. He knew more than I did. I had been told nothing, *nothing*. And I should be the heir. But *she* intends to cheat me of everything. She cheated me of my parents and, now, she intends to deprive me of my inheritance. Well, she's not going to!"

"And what about me?" Marcel asked in a cold voice. "What are you doing to me? This isn't yours; it's mine!"

"I haven't finished yet," Cèline cried. "Henri has double-crossed me, too; he said he had knowledge of the passage, but he was going on intuition. When

I decided to break away from him, he blackmailed me. He would have gone to the Countess and told her about our relationship, so we were forced to stay together. And then we thought of you. The rest, you know."

"And what can you gain by harming me?" Marcel said. "Père Cathé knows where I am tonight."

"That's easy," Cèline said. "I'll get rid of you all. Then I'll say Henri did it. He'll be found with the gun in his hand. None of you will be able to say anything and my story will be believed. I shall have public sympathy."

"You're behaving like a mad woman, Cèline," Marcel warned.

"Get back all of you," Cèline threatened. "I'm sorry to do this to you, Marcel, I quite liked you once I got to know you, but you can see the whole thing is hopeless. As for those two — " She stared at Henri, then Stella, who shrank back and grasped Marcel's cold hand.

"I'm sorry," he murmured, "I'm

going to try and get the gun off her."
He was raising his hand.

"Don't try anything, Marcel," she said. He was moving imperceptibly forward.

"You can shoot me if you like, Cèline, but let the girl go."

"How could anyone suspect a Parais of saying otherwise?" she snarled. "Arrogant to the last — and stupidly gallant. No, Marcel, I'm sorry, but this is the end of your treasure hunt."

"Listen, Cèline, don't you think you should check the treasure? How do you know the Nazis haven't filled the boxes with sand? Look, it's only the furniture that's exposed. Let me shine the torch inside and look." Stella saw her falter for a moment, prayed that Marcel's ploy would work. Cèline was still hesitating and, at that moment, Stella realised she was as mercenary as her aunt.

"Right, all of you, move back, back." They did very slowly and, soon, were pressing against the cases.

"Slowly, Stella, slowly," Marcel breathed. "When I pull open one of the cases, I'll try and black us out. It's our only chance."

"Open that big one there," Cèline said and her voice was thin and hard.

It was a very tall case, propped against the wall. Stella was praying silently as Henri held the lantern close and Marcel prised at the packing. The case wobbled with his efforts. After what seemed an age, the front was off.

Stella gasped. There, confronting the four of them, was the most glorious oil painting she had ever seen. The man in the picture was clad in full mediaeval armour. He stood in a forest landscape and, close to his side, pressed a magnificent hound wearing a small crown and a golden collar. The dog's forepaws were planted squarely on the white road that snaked towards the forest green.

"Roger!" Marcel cried. "The picture of Roger d'Artaigne!" They stood, mesmerised and in that tiny second, Marcel had flung himself towards Henri and dashed the storm lantern from his hand. There was the redness of flame — then blackness.

Stella didn't know what to do but stood, cowering in the dark, her only sense of direction the wind blowing down the passage upon her face.

She could hear Cèline's scream and a muffled thud. Next moment, they were all in a beam of light. Stella blinked.

"Marcel? Are you all right? Marcel?" She could have fainted with relief. He was holding the torch and the gun. Cèline was rising from the floor.

"Turn," he said and his voice was colder than the wind. "Come here, Stella, you'll be OK now. You — " He motioned to Henri. "Get over there with her." The man tried to remonstrate, but Marcel was unmerciful. "I couldn't trust you even though my grandfather trusted a Fasson!"

"What are you going to do with us, Parais? Leave me out of it. I've done nothing. She's the guilty one!" Henri blustered.

"Don't believe him, Marcel," Stella said. "I heard the way he threatened her. And it's his gun!"

"I know, Stella. Just come over here, please."

She came over obediently, her heart thumping, her head dizzy with what had just happened. They stood, confronting Cèline and Henri Fasson.

"What do you want me to do, Marcel?" she asked, hoping that he wouldn't leave her holding the weapon.

"I'd like you to go back along the passage and telephone the police. I'll stay with these two. Do you think you can do that?" She nodded. Suddenly, Cèline gave a step forward. She was smiling in a peculiar kind of way. Henri remained still, his face impassive.

"Keep back, Cèline," Marcel ordered, "or I'll shoot!"

"No, you won't shoot anyone, Parais," came a voice from behind and Cèline laughed out loud. Together, Marcel and

Stella turned. To the utter amazement of both, the speaker was standing, pointing a shotgun at Marcel's chest. It was the Countess Chard.

She was wearing black trousers and a sweater, and her elegant hairstyle had been replaced by a careless pony tail, which left wisps of grey blowing about her face. Her skin appeared to be stretched across the bone structure of her face like a skull hardly alive. Her mouth was a red gash where her lipstick had been smeared hurriedly. It was her eyes that Stella feared. They were bright and calculating — the only live things in that mask of a face.

"Back, Parais," she said, "with the others. Miss Foster, this is hardly a surprise. Back, all of you!"

"Put that down, Countess," Marcel said, "I still have the revolver."

"And I am still an excellent shot," she replied, "and if we shoot each other, I will spray the air with lead and then what injuries will that cause to the girl? Back! Throw away your pistol!"

"Oh, Aunt, thank goodness," Cèline cried, running forward suddenly and grasping Marcel's weapon. With a terrific bang, the shotgun went off, catching Cèline Chard full in the side and she toppled over. Marcel had fallen too and Stella screamed.

"Marcel, Marcel!" He was stirring, coming to. There was blood on his arm. He looked very white and was clutching at the deep graze. Cèline was moaning from where she lay on the floor. Henri was down, crouching for cover and the Countess was reloading. Stella went for the pistol, but Marcel shouted, "No. Stella, no, she'll kill you!" Stella wavered and then it was too late. The old woman was pointing the shotgun directly at her.

"He's right, Miss Foster." Stella drew back. "Now, miss, kick the weapon away, right away from you." She could do nothing but obey. "Now you can see to your lover."

The Countess motioned Stella, who

was looking for something to tie up the wound.

"What about her?" Stella cried. Cèline's blood was everywhere and she looked deathly white.

"Leave her to bleed to death!" was the reply.

"You can't do that," Marcel shouted. "You've still a chance. You can't kill the heir to Lange." He must have known what he was saying because the old Countess looked deathly grey. He took advantage of the situation and, bending over Cèline, he motioned to Stella.

"Get Henri's shirt and we'll try and staunch the blood flow."

Stella crept over to him, terrified the Countess would shoot her next.

"Please, Henri, do this for her," she begged.

Finally, he unbuttoned his shirt and gave it to Stella. She and Marcel ripped it into bandages as the old Countess watched impassively. Suddenly she began to speak in a low monotone, holding the shotgun loosely.

"The portrait of Roger d'Artaigne!" she muttered. "He looks like them all. All of them," she repeated. "Like you, like your father, like your precious grandfather. He could have had me if he wanted. I needed him, but he had to marry someone else. He was meant for me from the very beginning. We had everything in common, but he said he didn't love me.

"I was the good-looking twin, you know! My brother had no looks, nothing. He was a soft-hearted fool. He couldn't see they would have destroyed the Château if I hadn't co-operated. I wasn't going to lose my inheritance for anyone, least of all him. I was born first, you know. An hour before him. I was the heir. He was not — yet he would have had it all. My brother was willing to lose everything for some stupid idea of nobility," she said bitterly.

"The night before they took Parais away and tortured him, he confided everything in me — " Stella saw

Marcel look up at the old woman, then continue dressing Céline's wound. "He told me what he'd done with the treasure. He took me down the passage and showed me it all. And he made me promise never to tell. Said he'd love me if I kept it a secret. That when the war was over, we could be together, like we should have been all along. He said now his wife was dead he wanted a mother for his son. He was going to marry me. He thought that I could be trusted because of that. Marry me!" Her tone was bitter and full of disgust.

"He would have," Marcel said, rising from the floor. Stella got up with him. "We always keep our word. But how did you know where this passage was? If you're going to kill me you might as well let me into the secret." Stella knew Marcel was playing for time again.

"I was a very clever girl," the Countess replied.

"That night, after I left Parais, my brother and I had a terrible quarrel. I told him I had been into the secret

176

passage and that we should use it again like in the old days; that we should get away from the Nazis before they came for us.

"He demanded how I knew where it was and I told him about Parais' proposal. He was so glad for me. I begged him to tell me where our secret passageway began, appealed to his softness, told him that, as his twin, I had the right too. I won him round and he showed me how to operate the panel.

"I begged him to get away through the passage with his wife and child, but he would not. He was a fool. He preferred to be noble. He was afraid that the Nazis would take it out on the village. They did in any case; after they had shot him.

"I saved Céline's life and the Château by collaborating. I was not going to let it go for anything!"

"Not even for your brother?" Marcel said clearly.

"Not even for him! I told you, he was

a fool, not a Chard! And I'm not sorry at all. I did what I believed was right and I'm going to do it again. No-one is going to take the treasure from me. I was to have married a Parais and it would have been mine, anyway."

Stella could hardly bear to keep looking at the Countess's face. It had a twisted expression and there were red spots on her cheeks. Stella could hear her wheezy breath and she was afraid.

The Countess seemed to have finished and all the fight appeared to be dying. She looked wizened and shallow; a woman to be pitied rather than despised. Suddenly, she pulled up the heavy gun and pointed it directly at them. Stella could feel the wind on her face, blowing strongly through the secret passage. She put out her hand and caught Marcel's.

"This is it. We've had it," she said.

"We haven't, not yet. Don't shoot, Countess, don't shoot us. You'll be sorry. This afternoon a letter was delivered to Père Cathé saying if I wasn't out by daybreak he was to bring the police to the Château."

"I don't believe you, Parais. You're lying. No-one knows you are here."

"They do," Stella cried, "I took the message myself."

"You?" The Countess snapped, turning the gun on her. Stella shrank back against Marcel in terror. It was then a swift gust of wind swept through the passage and there was a creaking noise behind them. Stella and Marcel saw the Countess looking up in horror as the portrait of Roger d'Artaigne came crashing down out of its precarious bindings.

The Countess screamed and Marcel leaped out and grabbed the shotgun. Then she fell on her knees and remained crouching and hunched.

"Stay where you are!" Marcel shouted. Stella ran across to Céline again while Henri, seeing his opportunity, suddenly made a run for it.

Marcel, undecided whether to give

chase, was looking first at Stella, then at Céline.

"Go after him, Marcel. I'll be all right!" Stella was shaking with relief.

Then she heard other voices from far away down the secret passage, shouts and the sound of running feet.

"It must be Père Cathé and the police," she replied. "Thank goodness!"

They were suddenly held in the beam of powerful torchlights that made them blink. And then the torches were lowered and one of the men stepped forward. It was Johann, wearing an identity badge.

"Are you all right, Stella?" he asked, putting an arm about her shoulders.

"Yes, but what — ?"

"Enough for the moment. I see you are. I'm glad or Catherine would never have forgiven me!"

"I don't understand." Stella looked at Marcel. He shrugged his shoulders, but that tantalising smile was spreading over his face.

"I know you don't but, when we

have you safely outside, I'll explain."

They stood aside as the unconscious Céline was carried away on a stretcher; they watched silently as the Countess, now a shaken old woman, was led off down the passage by a policewoman and a detective.

"What about Henri?" Marcel asked.

"We have him too. In fact, a very successful evening," Detective Inspector Johann Manders replied. "Thanks to you, Stella."

It was only then that Stella realised just how worn out she was as she left the secret passage supported on one side by Marcel de Parais and the other by Johann.

* * *

Lange had never looked more beautiful to Stella than it did that lunch time. She and Catherine were seated outside under the pink and white striped awning of the best restaurant in the village.

There was the delicious aroma of French food wafting from the kitchens and two empty bottles of the best house wine sat on the table. Stella glanced through the open doors towards the two men, who were coming towards them.

"They get on really well, don't they?" Stella remarked as Marcel and Johann walked towards the table.

"Don't they just?" Catherine smiled. "Yet they hardly have anything in common!"

Johann and Marcel reached the table. The policeman turned to Catherine.

"Ready?" he said. She nodded, gathering her things.

"Now, remember, you two have a good afternoon," she instructed. "I'm sure you've plenty to talk about." She looked meaningfully at Stella. "Thank you, Marcel, it was a wonderful lunch."

"It was," Johann agreed, "and, I hope, we'll see you at the house for dinner before long!"

"You will," Marcel said, closing

his hand over Stella's. They watched Johann walk Catherine across the square. Stella looked up at the striped awning blowing in the breeze, remembering recent events.

"I still can't get over Johann being a policeman. It must have been nerve-racking working undercover at the Château Lange." Marcel was staring across and up the red cliff towards the great house.

"Not very nice, I would agree," he answered. "In fact, he aroused suspicions once or twice. But I'm still amazed that, before he died, my father had the chance to contact the police about the loss of his valuables. I wish I'd known. The operation nearly went tragically wrong."

"At least Johann and his men got to us in time. We could both be dead if he hadn't."

"I don't want to think about that," Marcel said, lifting her hand and kissing it. "Now I have everything I need."

"What do you mean?"

"The treasure." He was smiling at her. "My inheritance — especially Roger's picture — and a lovely friend."

"Thank you, Marcel," she replied, her eyes begging him to say more.

"Come on, then, if you want to see Artaigne." They rose and walked down the steps, leaving the tiny restaurant. Marcel's Alfa Romeo was parked just outside and he was most careful to hand her in to the car before going round the driver's side. Stella loved these old-fashioned gallantries and thought she could have no more perfect companion than Marcel.

There was another problem — she knew she was falling in love with him, but how did he feel? She was aware that he cared for her a lot, but she knew she wanted more. But now Marcel was heir to a tremendous fortune would he want her as well? Perhaps he would be looking for someone who had a lot of money — an aristocrat like himself?

"What's the matter?" he asked as they drove through the lanes. "Are you cold? I can put the hood up if you wish!"

"No, I'm not cold," she said. "It's lovely, Marcel — and there's nothing the matter."

She was unprepared for the sight of Artaigne. The Château's walls were still standing, but one could see the sky through the rows of windows.

"There's no roof, it was completely gutted," Marcel pointed out as they walked about inside the shell.

"What a task!" Stella said, looking at the piles of stone and the rotting timbers, all covered in brambles. "How are you going to do it, Marcel?"

"I don't know," he replied softly, "but I shall need some help!" Her heart was thumping as they walked on around the ruin. "That's where the lake is," he said, pointing eastwards. "We'll go there afterwards if you like. But it's all choked with weeds."

"All right," she called. She had come to a spot where some of the brambles had been cleared, the bushes were not as copious and the branches less thick.

She stood quietly, looking down at the floor. She was standing on the stone body of a hunting dog.

"Is this it, Marcel?" He was close behind her.

"Yes, somewhere under one of those dogs is the opening to Roger's passage. I can't remember just where. I'd have to step it out." She couldn't believe he was being serious when he said he could not remember.

"Anyway," he continued, "it doesn't really matter at the moment. I have other things on my mind." He paused, looked her straight in the eyes, then took her in his arms. She looked up at him and her gaze didn't waver.

"Such as, Marcel?" she asked, wanting nothing then except to stand there for ever in his arms. He was looking down at her, his eyes soft with feeling. He smiled at her expression.

"Such as, how long you're going to be in France. I hope it's a long time."

186

She felt dizzy at his nearness. "Oh, for quite a while, I should think. After all, you'll need someone to help you build all this up. Make it into a fairytale again."

His face was full of love.

"Thank you," he said and bent to kiss her. Afterwards, as they stood together breathless from that kiss, he added, "I could never have done it without your help."

They wandered along the side of the lake in the evening sunset. Somewhere in the ruins, pigeons were cooing a drowsy farewell to the day and the frogs were wakening to the coming night, croaking to each other from their hiding places at the water's edge.

As Stella and Marcel walked through the sweet-smelling grasses of summer, she was glad that the Château had yielded up its secret at last and one day, hopefully, would be a place of love and happiness again.

WITH SOMEBODY ELSE
Theresa Charles

Rosamond sets off for Cornwall with Hugo to meet his family, blissfully unaware of the shocks in store for her.

A SUMMER FOR STRANGERS
Claire Hamilton

Because she had lost her job, her flat and she had no money, Tabitha agreed to pose as Adam's future wife although she believed the scheme to be deceitful and cruel.

VILLA OF SINGING WATER
Angela Petron

The disquieting incidents that occurred at the Vatican and the Colosseum did not trouble Jan at first, but then they became increasingly unpleasant and alarming.

DOCTOR NAPIER'S NURSE
Pauline Ash

When cousins Midge and Derry are entered as probationer nurses on the same day but at different hospitals they agree to exchange identities.

A GIRL LIKE JULIE
Louise Ellis

Caroline absolutely adored Hugh Barrington, but then Julie Crane came into their lives. Julie was the kind of girl who attracts men without even trying.

COUNTRY DOCTOR
Paula Lindsay

When Evan Richmond bought a practice in a remote country village he did not realise that a casual encounter would lead to the loss of his heart.

ENCORE
Helga Moray

Craig and Janet realise that their true happiness lies with each other, but it is only under traumatic circumstances that they can be reunited.

NICOLETTE
Ivy Preston

When Grant Alston came back into her life, Nicolette was faced with a dilemma. Should she follow the path of duty or the path of love?

THE GOLDEN PUMA
Margaret Way

Catherine's time was spent looking after her father's Queensland farm. But what life was there without David, who wasn't interested in her?

HOSPITAL BY THE LAKE
Anne Durham

Nurse Marguerite Ingleby was always ready to become personally involved with her patients, to the despair of Brian Field, the Senior Surgical Registrar, who loved her.

VALLEY OF CONFLICT
David Farrell

Isolated in a hostel in the French Alps, Ann Russell sees her fiancé being seduced by a young girl. Then comes the avalanche that imperils their lives.

NURSE'S CHOICE
Peggy Gaddis

A proposal of marriage from the incredibly handsome and wealthy Reagan was enough to upset any girl — and Brooke Martin was no exception.

A DANGEROUS MAN
Anne Goring

Photographer Polly Burton was on safari in Mombasa when she met enigmatic Leon Hammond. But unpredictability was the name of the game where Leon was concerned.

PRECIOUS INHERITANCE
Joan Moules

Karen's new life working for an authoress took her from Sussex to a foreign airstrip and a kidnapping; to a real life adventure as gripping as any in the books she typed.

VISION OF LOVE
Grace Richmond

When Kathy takes over the rundown country kennels she finds Alec Stinton, a local vet, very helpful. But their friendship arouses bitter jealousy and a tragedy seems inevitable.

CRUSADING NURSE
Jane Converse

It was handsome Dr. Corbett who opened Nurse Susan Leighton's eyes and who set her off on a lonely crusade against some powerful enemies and a shattering struggle against the man she loved.

WILD ENCHANTMENT
Christina Green

Rowan's agreeable new boss had a dream of creating a famous perfume using her precious Silverstar, but Rowan's plans were very different.

DESERT ROMANCE
Irene Ord

Sally agrees to take her sister Pam's place as La Chartreuse the dancer, but she finds out there is more to it than dyeing her hair red and looking like her sister.

HEART OF ICE
Marie Sidney

How was January to know that not only would the warmth of the Swiss people thaw out her frozen heart, but that she too would play her part in helping someone to live again?

LUCKY IN LOVE
Margaret Wood

Companion-secretary to wealthy gambler Laura Duxford, who lived in Monaco, seemed to Melanie a fabulous job. Especially as Melanie had already lost her heart to Laura's son, Julian.

NURSE TO PRINCESS JASMINE
Lilian Woodward

Nick's surgeon brother, Tom, performs an operation on an Arabian princess, and she invites Tom, Nick and his fiancé to Omander, where a web of deceit and intrigue closes about them.

THE WAYWARD HEART
Eileen Barry

Disaster-prone Katherine's nickname was "Kate Calamity", but her boss went too far with an outrageous proposal, which because of her latest disaster, she could not refuse.

FOUR WEEKS IN WINTER
Jane Donnelly

Tessa wasn't looking forward to meeting Paul Mellor again — she had made a fool of herself over him once before. But was Orme Jared's solution to her problem likely to be the right one?

SURGERY BY THE SEA
Sheila Douglas

Medical student Meg hadn't really wanted to go and work with a G.P. on the Welsh coast although the job had its compensations. But Owen Roberts was certainly not one of them!

HEAVEN IS HIGH
Anne Hampson

The new heir to the Manor of Marbeck had been found. But it was rather unfortunate that when he arrived unexpectedly he found an uninvited guest, complete with stetson and high boots.

LOVE WILL COME
Sarah Devon

June Baker's boss was not really her idea of her ideal man, but when she went from third typist to boss's secretary overnight she began to change her mind.

ESCAPE TO ROMANCE
Kay Winchester

Oliver and Jean first met on Swale Island. They were both trying to begin their lives afresh, but neither had bargained for complications from the past.

CASTLE IN THE SUN
Cora Mayne

Emma's invalid sister, Kym, needed a warm climate, and Emma jumped at the chance of a job on a Mediterranean island. But Emma soon finds that intrigues and hazards lurk on the sunlit isle.

BEWARE OF LOVE
Kay Winchester

Carol Brampton resumes her nursing career when her family is killed in a car accident. With Dr. Patrick Farrell she begins to pick up the pieces of her life, but is bitterly hurt when insinuations are made about her to Patrick.

DARLING REBEL
Sarah Devon

When Jason Farradale's secretary met with an accident, her glamorous stand-in was quite unable to deal with one problem in particular.

THE PRICE OF PARADISE
Jane Arbor

It was a shock to Fern to meet her estranged husband on an island in the middle of the Indian Ocean, but to discover that her father had engineered it puzzled Fern. What did he hope to achieve?

DOCTOR IN PLASTER
Lisa Cooper

When Dr. Scott Sutcliffe is injured, Nurse Caroline Hurst has to cope with a very demanding private case. But when she realises her exasperating patient has stolen her heart, how can Caroline possibly stay?

A TOUCH OF HONEY
Lucy Gillen

Before she took the job as secretary to author Robert Dean, Cadie had heard how charming he was, but that wasn't her first impression at all.

ROMANTIC LEGACY
Cora Mayne

As kennelmaid to the Armstrongs, Ann Brown, had no idea that she would become the central figure in a web of mystery and intrigue.

THE RELENTLESS TIDE
Jill Murray

Steve Palmer shared Nurse Marie Blane's love of the sea and small boats. Marie's other passion was her step-brother. But when danger threatened who should she turn to — her step-brother or the man who stirred emotions in her heart?

ROMANCE IN NORWAY
Cora Mayne

Nancy Crawford hopes that her visit to Norway will help her to start life again. She certainly finds many surprises there, including unexpected happiness.

UNLOCK MY HEART
Honor Vincent

When Ruth Linton, a young widow with three children, inherits a house in the country, it seems to be the answer to her dreams. But Ruth's problems were only just beginning . . .

SWEET PROMISE
Janet Dailey

Erica had met Rafael in Mexico, where their relationship had been brief but dramatic. Now, over a year later in Texas, she had met him again — and he had the power to wreck her life.

SAFARI ENCOUNTER
Rosemary Carter

Jenny had to accept that she couldn't run her father's game park alone; so she let forceful Joshua Adams virtually take over. But Joshua took over her heart as well!

SHADOW DANCE
Margaret Way

When Carl Danning sent her to interview Richard Kauffman, Alix was far from pleased — but the assignment led her to help Richard repair the situation between him and his ex-wife.

WHITE HIBISCUS
Rosemary Pollock

"A boring English model with dubious morals," was how Count Paul Santana Demajo described Emma. But what about the Count's morals, and who is Marianne?

STARS THROUGH THE MIST
Betty Neels

Secretly in love with Gerard van Doordninck, Deborah should have been thrilled when he asked her to marry him. But he only wanted a wife for practical not romantic reasons.